Parting the Veil

PARTING THE VEIL
Stories from a Mormon Imagination

Phyllis Barber

SIGNATURE BOOKS / SALT LAKE CITY

COVER DESIGN BY BRIAN BEAN

NOTE: "Bread for Gunnar" first appeared in *Weber Studies* 10 (Fall 1993), in a special issue on "Tradition and the Individual Talent in Contemporary Mormon Letters"; "Devil Horse," in *New Hampshire College Journal* 12 (Spring 1995); "Dust to Dust," in *Dialogue: A Journal of Mormon Thought* 27 (Winter 1994); "The Fiddler and the Wolf," in *Sunstone* 18 (Apr. 1995), where it won second prize in the 1993 Brookie and D. K. Brown Memorial Fiction Contest; "Ida's Sabbath," in a different version, in *Sunstone* 8 (May-June 1983), as second prize winner in the 1983 D. K. Brown Memorial Fiction Contest; "Mormon Levis," which won first prize in the 1996 Brookie and D. K. Brown Memorial Fiction Contest, in *Quarterly West* (Twentieth Anniversary Issue), Autumn/ Winter 1996-97; "Prophet by the Sea," in *Dialogue: A Journal of Mormon Thought* 27 (Fall 1994); "Spirit Babies," *Quarterly West*, Summer/Fall 1994; "The Whip," which won second prize in the 1986 Utah Fine Arts Literary Competition, in *Dialogue: A Journal of Mormon Thought* 20 (Winter 1987); and "Wild Sage," which received Special Mention in *Pushcart Prize XIII*, first in *Dialogue: A Journal of Mormon Thought* 20 (Summer 1987), and later in *Beloit Fiction Journal* 9 (1994). "The Boy and the Hand" and "A Brief History of Seagulls: A Trilogy with Notes" appear here for the first time.

Parting the Veil: Stories from a Mormon Imagination was printed on acid-free paper and manufactured in the United States of America.

Library of Congress Cataloging-in-Publication Data
Barber, Phyllis,
    Parting the veil : stories from a Mormon imagination / by Phyllis Barber.
       p.   cm.
    ISBN 1-56085-120-2 (pbk.)
    1. Mormons—West (U.S.)—Social life and customs—Fiction. I. Title.
    PS3552.A59197P37   1999
    813'.54—dc21   98-472994
                                         CIP

To my sisters

Kathryn Gold and Elaine McIver

and my brother

H. Stephen Nelson

Contents

Preface and Acknowledgements

Raised in the dry deserts and sheer-walled canyon country of the Colorado River plateau—fermenting ground for many kinds of dreams—I watched my father anoint my sister's head with oil, lay his hands on the crown of her head, and bless her to recover from rheumatic fever. And she did.

There is something about Mormonism that keeps bringing me back to its roots, something about the power of the miraculous I knew so intimately as a child.

I was always fascinated by Sunday school stories of Joseph Smith's visions and the angel leading him to gold plates buried in a hill. In sacrament meeting I heard about the Three Nephites—three men granted their wish to live forever by Jesus when he appeared in the Americas—and how they rescued people in harm's way before disappearing in thin air. At the dinner table, I heard how a World War II soldier's temple garments protected him from a bullet. Underneath quilt frames, playing with my mother's shoelaces, I heard how unborn spirits talked to women in the night and asked to receive a body.

When I was a child, it was as common to think of an angel appearing by my bed as it was to drink orange juice for breakfast. As an adult, I experienced the white light of the Holy Ghost pouring into my mind and comforting me at an especially low moment of my life. This belief in the parting of the veil between heaven and earth has never been far from me, though there have been those moments in time when my innocence was, as all innocence must be, challenged—moments when I watched my idealism fall and my faith crumble. Real life was too disparate from the pretty picture.

But, ultimately, the web is wide. The canvas is broad. God moves in mysterious ways, and a mystery is a mystery—protean, awe-inspiring. God is the quixotic, the ineffable, the Great Possibility, still and always beyond the reach of finite understanding. And yet we humans are always reaching. All but one married couple in my ancestral lineage of the 1800s crossed the great American plains to Zion, walked behind handcarts, and rode in conestogas (one serving as wagonmaster for early church leaders), all because they believed in something that moved them to unfathomable exploits. What is this something that moved men and women to give up all they had, to leave comfortable homes, to separate from families, to build an empire in the name of God? Had the veil parted for them? Could they see into the Mystery?

The Mormonism I most identify with begins where the Church of Jesus Christ of Latter-day Saints did—with Joseph Smith and his visionary ideas that have given my own imagination access to infinite possibility: social and economic communitarianism, plural marriage, vicarious baptism for the dead, conversations with heavenly beings, free-flowing consideration of any meritorious idea (including Freemasonry and the plurality of gods), the literal building of a kingdom of God on earth, and much more. Often baffled by the interstellar scope of Joseph Smith's vision and the relative lack of interest in the man and his work, especially outside the culture, I was pleased to read *The American Religion* in which noted critic Harold Bloom boldly recognizes Smith's creative genius. "Latter-day Saints, however much their Church may have had to stray from his paths, have been almost alone in apprehending the greatness of Joseph Smith. An entire century after the Mormon repudiation of plural marriage, their prophet remains without honor among most of his countrymen."

My main point of intersection with Mormonism is with the beginnings—the primitive, innocent, robust religion. It is in the places where people, not unlike Joseph Smith seeking an answer to his prayers, have original and firsthand encounters with the divine. It's the mystical interaction with the unknown, the human reaching out to touch the finger of God, the supernatural.

As South Africans say, "The bird sings the way it is beaked." Not so surprisingly, with this collection of stories (some of which are drawn from Utah folklore and Mormon history, and others of which are more contemporary portraits of people caught by the Mormon ideal), I'm singing bits and pieces of themes familiar to my ear. And, as much as I vacillate between the need to know and the need to doubt, I can't help telling stories that wrestle with the suspicion of a thin veil fluttering nearby.

Many heartfelt thanks to the Fife Folklore Collection at Utah State University, the Utah State Historical Society, Mormon storytellers who carry on the tales and legends, Writers at Work in Park City, Utah, and to students and faculty in the Vermont College MFA in Writing Program for their enthusiastic support.

Special thanks to Kathryn Gold for her perceptive criticism; Gladys and Richard Swan for their intellectual comprehension; Neila Seshachari, editor of *Weber Studies*, for her belief in the richness, imagination, and creativity of "Mormon Literature;" Chris, Jeremy, and Brad Barber for being there and still believing; and to David Barber, Paul Swenson, Connie Chard, Gordon Weaver, Francois Camoin, Rod Ondler, and Gary Bergera at Signature Books.

There is, apart from mere intellect, in the make-up
of ... human identity, a wondrous something that
realizes without argument, frequently without
what is called education ... an intuition of the ab-
solute balance, in time and space, of the whole of
this multifariousness, this revel of fools, and in-
credible make-believe and general unsettledness,
we call *the world*, a soul-flight of that divine clue
and unseen thread which holds ... all history and
time, and all events, however trivial, however mo-
mentous, like a leashed dog in the hand of the
hunter. [Of] such soul-sight and root-centre for
the mind mere optimism explains only the surface.

—WALT WHITMAN

The Whip

Headed west to Utah, Brother and Sister Gustavson pushed their handcart for many miles singing, "Some must push and some must pull," before their miracle happened. They inherited a wagon—all in the moment a hand could turn from side to side. It was a conestoga.

The former owner, a woman who had left her husband for God and Zion, lost her only child in a drowning pond. A few minutes after the accident, she decided to follow this child into heaven. "Children are undefiled," she said. "Pure candidates for the celestial kingdom. I'll hold onto her hand."

So there were a wagon and two oxen where there had only been a squeaky handcart. And, best of all, at least in the eyes of Karl Gustavson, was the braided whip left on the wagon seat. There it was. Coiled on that high shelf of a wooden seat.

Those who knew Karl when he was a boy knew he liked to play with whips, to crack them, to use them to lasso bottles on fence posts. Just when he mastered the art of fly-swatting with his whip, however, his mother decided enough was enough. "It's that cracking sound that I love," he told his mother, but she meant enough was enough when she said so.

So while Hilma Gustavson loaded her loose assortment of dishes into a small cupboard left in a corner, pretending the wagon was her first real home in America, Karl practiced. He remembered everything, almost as if his whip had been taken away only an hour before. Hilma heard the cracking and snapping and whirring in the air just outside of the wagon, but nothing mattered except this small box of a home. She folded her blankets over her alfalfa and corn seed, tied her looking glass to a wagon brace, then sat on the high wooden seat with her hands folded.

"Let's join the others, dear," she said, sitting like a priestess of the highest kingdom of glory, settling a pillow around her ample hips. Brother and Sister Gustavson said good-bye to their handcart and joined in prayer for continued safe journeying. Karl whipped the oxen politely, and they were off for Utah once again.

Before Karl and Hilma went to sleep that night, he found every fly in the vicinity that might bother them while they slept. He flicked the whip and snapped every fly into oblivion. Before long he got so he could lash every winged creature before Hilma could say, "Karl, why must we have flies on top of everything else. Is there no rest?" After a few weeks Karl began to coil the whip under his pillow, touching it every time he turned onto his stomach.

At first, Hilma rejoiced in Karl's unusual ability. She laughed at his quickness and told him he was the best protector in all the world. After all, with his whip, he could move the oxen, even when they didn't want to lift a hoof. He kept flies and their sticky feet out of their dinner—there was much too little to share—and he prevented the moths from gumming up their lantern. Many things were good about Karl's new skill.

About this time, however, he started taking the whip to campfire dances on Saturday night where he showed everyone how he could flick a fly from the nose of a sleeping dog. At first, Hilma thought this was unique and allowed herself a little boasting. But when he took the whip to Sunday meetings and told the brethren he would protect them from any insects that buzzed them while they were speaking from God to the congregation, Hilma began to fold her blankets twenty-six times a day, count her alfalfa and corn seeds, and polish the glass on the dish cupboard even though it was unnecessary, all for an excuse to stay out of sight.

"My dear husband, how about a new pastime?"

"Look at me, Hilma. Look how I can make this whip fill with humps!" He lashed the whip and made it ripple like the skin of a running horse.

"But," Hilma insisted, "you've mastered everything there is to master with this whip. Find something else to do."

Their conversations started to have long pauses. Hilma could not keep from the subject of the whip and how Karl should lay it to rest. Karl could not keep from surveying his immediate territory for any kind of flying object, even floating cottonwood seeds and specks of dust. He could barely finish a sentence. His eyes and mind wandered from every conversation.

Hilma thought of hiding the whip, but the wagon was small and nothing could stay hidden for long. She thought of burying it at the edge of the wagon trail, but because Karl had become rather unpopular with the other pioneers, he was always at her side.

Hilma started to pray at night. "Dear God. The whip. It is not good. All of thy little creatures are unsafe. I promise I'll never complain about flies again if thou will aid me in a solution. Karl is forgetting about thee. His mind must be single to thy glory. Amen."

She never knew quite how it happened, but one afternoon when she was dicing a potato that had traveled many miles with them, but was about to be eaten up by a growing white root system, she saw Karl's whip curled neatly on the axle of the wagon wheel. He had gone to priesthood meeting without his whip. Surely God had heard her prayers. She didn't even think about her actions, she swore later—it was divine intercession that led her. She laid the whip across the cutting board that was balanced on her knees, and she diced, hacked, chopped, and sawed. One half inch at a time, she chopped it into pieces resembling jerked meat—a luxury. They hadn't had any in so long. As she shortened the whip, she almost started to believe in it herself.

She peered into the boiling water and felt the steam rise in her face. Steam and smoke from the fire. She felt like a witch over a cauldron, but knew she was doing God's will as she scraped the diced whip into the boiling water. And it boiled and boiled until the whip was limp and soft and edible.

"Your dinner." Hilma handed a steaming bowl of soup to her husband.

"Where did you find the beef, my resourceful Hilma?" He chewed slowly, his teeth unaccustomed to anything but root vegetables and bread. "I'm a blessed man."

Hilma smiled without showing her teeth. "God provides."

"Amen." He chewed with his eyes closed, remembering far away times when he had herring, rye bread, chopped onions, and capers on his table. "You are so good to me." But then he stopped chewing abruptly. "A fly, Hilma! Quick, my whip?"

"I'm sure you have it with you, Karl."

"I don't see it anywhere." He looked inside the wagon, inside the dish cupboard, under the blankets, under the wagon. He checked the oxen. He looked in the cookpots. His lip quivered like it did as a boy when his mother took it away. "Hilma. My whip. It's gone!"

Hilma pulled Karl to her side, put her large arm around him, and covered his knees with her woolen shawl. "You know everything about that whip. You know how it feels, its sharp sound when it cracks. So you wouldn't need to hold it in your hand ever again and it would still be yours."

Karl thought about that for a minute. "No one can take it away from me?"

"No one," said Hilma. She patted his knuckles.

Karl hunched over to contemplate and finally shrugged a grudging acceptance. "If it had to happen, I'm glad it was on a day when we had a real supper. May I have another bowl of soup?"

As Hilma ladled the soup with meat into his clay bowl, Karl complimented himself for choosing Hilma as a wife for eternity. "God knew what I needed and sent you, Hilma. The wagon, too."

She smiled quietly, rocked on her soft buttocks, and tried to keep her teeth from showing. "God is good," she said.

Spirit Babies

Delta patted her lips with a paper napkin, crumpled it, and swished it into the basketball net clamped to the top of the wastebasket. She pulled her hefty arms from the counter, eased off her stool, and rinsed her bowl under the tap. "Give me your cup, J. L. I'll rinse it out."

He drained the bottom, handed her the mug, and then leaned against the kitchen counter, his arms folded. "Okay, tell me one more time. What happens when you see him?"

"Well, the first dream, he looks like he might be a gymnast when he comes down at least a thousand stairs, little old baby, half crawling, half rolling down those stairs. He's laughing all the way, though. In between the crawling and the rolling, he's reaching his arms up to me and saying, 'Mama, Mama.' He's wearing a little white robe, but it barely covers him. That's how I can tell it's a him, you know. Then, instead of finishing up with those thousand stairs, he starts to fly and roll like an airplane. He cruises over my head, close to my hair so I can feel some of it lifting up with the electricity, and says, 'I'm waiting, Mama.' I mean, what can I say? I can't sleep for all the things this child says to me in the night. Sometimes I think he might even be a prophet."

"Why doesn't he come see me?" J. L. pulled up his Levis by the belt loops again and tucked his shirt in the back. "I've got something to do with this, I think. I'm the man of the house."

Delta turned her glowing face to her husband. "You sure are, honey." Her auburn hair was backlit by the square of morning light in the window, a pale fire smoldering on top of Mt. Delta.

Suddenly, he smiled like a sunning snake, happy with the first day after winter. "Delta," he said, looking at his wife with that bashful look he sometimes had. "You sure are pretty when God talks to you. Seven kids, and I still feel my blood rising in me. You just here in the kitchen in your sweats and high tops. I did a good thing when I chose you."

"You didn't choose me, Johnny Lester Bradford. We chose each other before we ever came to this earth. Don't you remember?"

"Well, sort of." J. L. squinched his left eye and puckered his lips in thought. His straw brown hair was tinted pure sunlight, his eyebrows too. "Tell you the truth, Delta, I don't remember seeing you before that night at the Milton Ward's potluck dinner, eighteen years ago, you pouring water in glasses and wearing the brightest yellow-like sunshine."

"Johnny Lester," Delta said, cozying her backside against his belt buckle and tucking her seventy-two-inch body under his chin. "Put your arms around me, honey. Just hold me and believe with me."

He wrapped her tightly against his body and rocked her with a little Motown. "My girl, talkin' 'bout my girl ..." He stroked the letters on her purple sweatshirt, most especially the "O" that covered her breast.

"You better get your body off to work, J. L. Night's a better time for taking care of dreams." Reaching over her shoulder, she flipped his ear, then turned and applied a half-nelson, something he'd taught her once when she wanted to break into high school wrestling. She wanted to be called Delta Dawn, the Rumbler, or better yet, Thunder of the Morning.

J. L. jabbed a mild elbow into her ribs and bridged out of the hold. "I'll think about you on my long haul to Vegas today. I'll be back to-morrow night, then we'll talk about this baby in your dream." He popped the Zion's National Park cap on his head and settled it just so, pulled on the rim, then curved it between two hands. "Why don't you dream a little dream of me?" he whispered and winked as he pulled the door closed behind him.

Delta Ray Bradford untwisted the orange-covered wire on the

bread bag. "Dream a little dream of me," she half-sang underneath her breath, lining up ten pieces of whole wheat bread on the counter, slathering each with canola margarine, light Mayo, tuna fish, and topping with pickles, sprouts, and Bibb lettuce. She counted out five brown paper bags, shook them open, then peeled ten carrots and sliced them into sticks. Fruit rolls. Cranapple juice in a box with the straw attached to the side. A piece of homemade carrot cake made with whole wheat flour Delta had ground herself.

She sat at the kitchen counter and pulled a worn box of magic markers out of the cluttered drawer. In her best Palmer's penmanship, she wrote out five notes—one for each of her school children, each one slightly different from the next. "Keep a smile on your face," she wrote with a green felt tip pen. "Remember who loves you," she wrote on another piece of paper. "Love one another."

She lined the notes up side by side and, using the yellow marker, made her secret mother symbol on each one: the figure-eight sign for infinity. Then she plucked the red pen out of the dog-eared, gray-cornered box. Uncapping it with a flourish, she patiently drew the outline and filled in the contours of five pairs of generous lips, then sealed each note with a kiss of her own.

When Delta Ray arrived at Midtown Mart that afternoon, she told her three-year-old, Tara Sue, to sit quietly in the basket while she secured Jared in the seat of the grocery cart with the pink nylon strap provided by Midtown. He was a climber of the first order, and she knew if he escaped the cart, there was no telling what he'd find on the floor. Squashed grapes. Ignored pennies. Dirt, plenty of it. His little hands would reach up to the lip of the produce shelf and pull tomatoes and oranges in a shower upon himself. Then he'd squash those ripe tomatoes in his hands, red pulp dripping down his plump arms, and laugh like he'd invented laughing.

Secretly, Delta Ray was proud of him and his ways, but she knew better than to show this joy in public. As she pulled the buckle tight around Jared's pudgy waist, she heard whispers behind her.

"Do you think Delta Ray's pregnant again?" she heard good old VerJean whisper to Sandy, one of the check-out girls. "She always looks as if she might be pregnant." Delta Ray busied herself with pulling a coloring book and crayons out of her gigantic Mexican straw bag. "You color those animals any old color you want, Tara Sue," she said, handing her the book and the yellow box with green stripes, "but just stay put in that basket. No standing while we're in the store. Get the message?"

Tara Sue shook her head vigorously with a good-girl yes. But then Delta Ray heard busybody VerJean again. "Delta's got a lentil for a brain."

Usually, Delta tried not to use her strength in public, but today she almost shot a threatening look in VerJean's direction. Delta could be imposing, being exactly six feet tall. Her chest was, after all, except for her breasts, a close replica of her father's. He'd been a linebacker in the regional high school all-star game once upon a time. But Delta repressed the impulse, pretending to be more interested in the front page of the newsprint advertiser in her hands. It featured a picture of a swordfish with a broad-bladed pirate's sword drawn in place of its snout. Then she sucked in her stomach muscles and lifted her chin.

"I'm pregnant with the spirit," Delta Ray said slowly with emphasis as she glided the grocery cart toward Sandy's check-out stand and VerJean. "Blown up like a dirigible, flying for God." She stopped in front of the two women, smiled as if she were the Mother of Cosmic Content, and held Jared's chin in her hand. "My blessed ones," she said as she kissed his eyebrow and patted Tara Sue's blond curls. "Angel babies."

VerJean didn't look up. She scribbled a note on her shopping list, all the time acting as if she didn't have a mouth on her. Sandy acted busy as a bee. Dressed in a red-check Western Days shirt with a red-fringed yoke and wearing a cut-out cowboy hat badge with "Sandy-O" written across the hatband, she plumped open a paper bag and waved politely at Delta Ray pushing her cart into the pasta aisle.

Muzak was playing "Let It Be." Delta Ray hummed. She plucked a thin box of fettucine from the shelf and tried to balance it on Jared's head. He laughed. "Speaking words of wisdom, let it be," she sang.

At that very moment, however, she happened to see one of the laws of the land being shattered like a stone tablet against rock. At the end of the aisle, right by the expensive nuts, she saw Jeff Jex's hand dart out of his pocket and grab a handful of cellophane tubes of cashews. Then another handful. Then some pistachios. Like lightning, he hid them in the deep pockets of his baggy beige shorts, faster than Delta

Ray could sing the last "let it be."

"Hey you," she shouted. "What do you think you're doing?

Delta Ray's cart sang down the aisle, the lopsided wheel adding its own rhythm to the Muzak. She whizzed past long grain rice, Chinese noodles, water chestnuts, and bamboo shoots. Ca-chunk, ca-chunk, the wheel, the spaces between the floor tiles. Ca-chunk. Let It Be. God's own chariot winging out of the sky, landing on Aisle 6, catching young Jeff Jex in an unsavory act.

"Okay," Delta Ray said, her voice booming out of her expansive chest. "What's going on here?"

Young Jex gave Delta Ray the finger. "Fuck you," he said, his lips lingering over the "f" of the fuck, his delivery slow and impudent.

Delta Ray's eyes grew wider than a full moon on a clear night. "You don't say that to me, young man," she said, her fists on her generous hips. "Nobody speaks that way to me, especially not a thief."

"You cretin." Jeff Jex stood there with fists jammed into his thighs, his voluminous shorts low on his hips, his black hair jelled Elvis-style.

"If I were you, young Jex, I'd be getting my running shoes on and fast."

"You're a joke, Mrs. Bradford, just like all your snot-nosed kids. Don't you care about pollution?"

Delta Ray hit faster than a jet. God's jet arrayed in purple sweat pants, a purple sweatshirt that said "Milton Boosters" across her broad chest. Kamikaze. Ke-yi. She tied up Jeff Jex with something close to a full nelson, though she kept it this side of legal. "I won't break your neck, you pompous little shit, but you better understand one thing."

Jeff Jex was white. Sweat poured down his temples and pooled underneath the lobe of his ear. His slick black hair fell like two commas over the sides of his face—two hanks of hair shaken out of place by Delta Ray Bradford, uncrowned Milton Wrestler of the Year. In one quick motion, he pulled the three packages of cashews out of his pocket, dropped them on the floor, and kicked them with the toe of his scuffed black cowboy boot. "Sexual harassment," Jeff screamed. "Get this nymphomaniac off me."

Jared was chanting "Mommy, Mommy, Mommy." Tara Sue was climbing up and over the edge of the basket to help her mother. Somehow, Delta Ray's maternal antennae could feel her daughter climbing, balancing, one leg on the outside of the cart, her chin scraping over the hard metal rods of the basket. Releasing the young man, she whirled around to see Tara Sue falling, landing, her chin red. She whirled just in time to hear the sound of Tara Sue's head on the hard floor, the cherubic face still and doll-like and China-painted on the floor of the Midtown Market. Tara Sue: A picture of serenity framed with pieces of tile smudged with the dirt from people's shoes, their black heel marks, the crushed berries falling out of carts, to the floor, bruised beneath someone's careless heel.

"Tara Sue. My strawberry princess. My apple." Delta Ray kneeled over her daughter.

"Mommy, Mommy." Jared never stopped.

"Call 911," she yelled to a stock boy carrying a box down the aisle.

"Right away." The boy slid the box to the floor and ran toward the store's office. A stranger with black rimmed glasses stopped her cart next to Delta's and tried to comfort Jared. Jeff Jex froze in suspended animation, undecided about which way to move.

Delta Ray rolled onto her hips and cupped Tara Sue's face in her hands. She closed her eyes and ears to all the sounds around her and, in her mind, watched her own body rise up out of the pasta aisle to the safe place where nobody could ever be hurt. She watched Tara Sue rise with her as she pushed aside the walls of the clouds. "You'll bless my baby, won't you?" she asked the first angel she saw, who happened to be carrying a trumpet. "You'll bless and protect my littlest angel girl and make her hair keep curling and her eyes keep shining like stars, won't you please?"

Sitting smack dab in the middle of Aisle 6 of Midtown Market, Delta rocked her baby love in her arms and finger-combed her fine-spun hair all the time she talked to the angel. "'Delta,' she used to call to me before she was born. 'Please let me come to your house, Delta Ray. Please.'" Delta looked up into the crystal-like eyes of the angel who lifted his trumpet to his lips and blew a long mournful sound that filled the heavens. It was one long, sad note. He blew and blew the same blue note as tears streamed out of Delta's eyes and someone handed her a linen handkerchief and told her to blow her nose.

And then the paramedics were there, the gray stretcher, the sound of velcro ripping apart after the blood pressure check, dark blue shirts with gold patches on their sleeves, serious looks on their faces, Jeff Jex standing beside them, eyes blank like post holes, the commas of his hair still hanging forward over his ears.

"She's got a weak pulse," one of the paramedics said. "Concussion, probably. Better get her over to General."

Delta Ray followed the dark blue shirts into the red and white ambulance, into the wide-open back doors, gauges, timeless clocks, upside down bottles of clear fluid.

As the doors to the ambulance were closing, she saw Jeff Jex standing in the doorway of Midtown Market, surrounded by pots of pinkish coral geraniums, lobelia that was bluer than the angel's trumpet solo, and the gray leaves of dusty miller. She saw the dark blue and the gray more than anything at that moment, until they became ribbons of color draping across Tara Sue's white face. Tara Sue, the only thing her five senses could recognize. It wasn't until two blocks later, as the ambulance pulled underneath the awning of the hospital, that her brain finally registered the whole of the picture she'd seen. Jeff Jex had been holding Jared by the hand. Jared was crying. "Mommy, Mommy." Jeff Jex was reaching into his pocket, pulling out a dollar bill, handing it to Delta's two-year-old, kneeling down to beg Jared to stop crying. VerJean was watching through Midtown's glass door, leaning forward, her neck stretched, peering.

The night was filled with crickets rubbing their legs—crickets and the smell of the stockyard and the irrigation water on the outlying pastures of hay tall enough to mow. The moon silvered the aluminum frame on the bedroom window and made the almost asleep Delta Ray think of stripes. The flag at the post office. Beach towels through the wire fence of the town pool. The black and white of the neighborhood's picket fences as the ambulance sped by. The red stripe on the hospital floor, guiding her to the emergency room. A brown stripe on the wall. A green stripe above the brown stripe. Tara Sue. Her angel baby. Stripes of light through the venetian blinds across Tara Sue's face as she lay in the hospital room, barely breathing.

And she remembered Bishop Sohm entering the room with his two counselors, his blue and white striped shirt, his farmer's tan face with the white stripe where his hat had been. The anointment. The rubbing of the oil in Tara's curls. The stripes of all the men's fingers gentle on Tara Sue's head. "By the power of the Holy Melchizedek priesthood," Bishop Sohm speaking, "I lay my hands upon your head for the purpose of giving you a blessing."

Little Tara. Life low in her. Poor in body. Bishop Sohm calling earnestly to God, "Save this baby. Give her life." The men lifting their straw hats back on their heads, smiling contented smiles, shaking hands. "God bless you and Tara, Delta Ray," the bishop was saying. "The spirit tells me she's going to be fine. Say hi to J. L. when he gets back from his run to Vegas. We need him out on the welfare farm when things are right with Tara here." The men leaving. The door closing. Delta Ray staring down at Tara Sue, life still shallow in her. Delta Ray, mumbling prayers, intoning her child's name, "Tara Sue, my baby," as if the sound, the calling, would bring Tara back. Tara Sue, still quiet, Delta Ray placing her own fingers on Tara's head, "By the power of Jesus, who I love, I bless you, Tara Sue Bradford. Blast out of this Chicken Wing the Reaper's got you locked in. Bridge out. Break free, my angel baby." Tara finally stirring, finally turning her head to the left side, finally holding Delta Ray's finger in her hand.

And now, her head crushed into a pillow, her eyes staring at the ceiling, Delta Ray listened to the crickets and smelled the irrigation water and waited for J. L.'s rig to pull into the yard. She held Tara Sue in her arms. Tara, still alive, still a three-year-old full of delicate life, still the same Tara Sue Bradford who tomorrow would be laughing and coloring butterflies on everyone's lunch sacks and watching her older sisters taking dancing lessons at Miss Jean's Studio for Acrobatics and Tap.

And as Delta Ray held Tara as closely as possible and felt her curls under her chin, the sound of the crickets hypnotized her. Their steady rhythm walked her into the world of dreams. She slipped through the dark tunnel of sleep and into a place with hundreds of children dressed in white, tons of children, seas of children. "Delta Ray," she heard them singing. "We're coming. We're coming. Won't you let us live with you, Delta Ray?"

The children were dancing, shaking their hands in the air, some of them slapping the skins of ghost tambourines. "Give us bodies, Delta Ray. Let us be." Delta saw a familiar one doing a few flips and balancing on a beam of light. "My turn next, Delta Ray." And then J. L.

danced into the dream. He arched his back, spread his arms, and grinned at her as Motown amped through the heavenly dance hall. "My girl. Talkin' 'bout my girl." Music filled every nook and cranny of her dream until she felt something on her shoulder.

"Delta," J. L. whispered, tapping her shoulder. "Delta. I'm home." He sat carefully on the bed, tossed his Zion's National Park hat on one of the dresser mirror's spindles, lifted his wife's hair off her ear, and kissed her cheek.

"That you, J. L.?" she asked, groggy. "I just saw you dancing in my dream."

"Forget dancing. I'm ready to wrestle, Delta Ray, woman of my dreams." He smiled, his lips chalked white in a stripe of moonlight, and put his arm underneath her head. "If God says we should have more babies, then I'm willing to do my part. You're a good woman, Delta, and when I prayed last night, God told me he'd provide if we helped him out. I even saw that gymnast baby in my dreams. He did a few flips and said, 'Hi, J. L. Sure hope to be seeing you soon.'" J. L. was smiling large and wide. "I felt real good about him talking to me. Came just before I went to sleep. Cute little tyke."

"There's so many," Delta Ray mumbled and rolled her head from side to side. "I saw hundreds and thousands of them."

"That's a lot of spirit babies, I'd say. But maybe we can assist one more of them, my honey love. Let me put Tara Sue to bed and then, maybe, we can come up with a new hold of some kind." He wiggled his eyebrows like Groucho.

Delta Ray tightened her hold on Tara. "I just want to hold Tara Sue for now, J. L. Feel her hair against my Adam's apple, glossy like it is. We almost lost her yesterday. Grocery cart. She fell. But, just as bad, I left Jared in the cart. We were lucky Jeff Jex was there to unbuckle him and VerJean was there to take him to her house. Even if he did call me a cretin and a nymphomaniac."

"A what? He always was a smart-assed little kid. A what?"

"Maybe he's right, J. L. Maybe I'm foolish about these spirit babies. Maybe I'm only a dumbcretinympho ..." She pulled the pillow out from under her head and pushed it into her face to drown her words.

"Is my Delta Ray losing heart?" J. L. lifted the corner of the pillow, then the pillow itself. "Come out of there. Escape time. Have I ever seen my Delta Ray back down under pressure? Nosirree."

"I wish he would have called me something different," Delta said, curling fetal.

"But people don't understand the higher law like you do. They don't understand there's always room for one more. Let me take Tara to bed. Let me love you, Delta. Don't feel bad."

J. L. lifted Tara Sue into his arms, rocked her side to side as her chin rested on his shoulder, and kissed the tip of her ear.

"People could be right about me," Delta said staring up at the ceiling. "Let me hold her a little longer." Delta stretched long on her back and held out both arms like two stumps of trees in the dark shadows of the room. "Nobody can take away our Tara, can they J. L.?"

"No, honey." He eased Tara Sue back into her mother's arms, Tara limp with sleep. "I don't like seeing my warrior with the blues, though. Bridge out, like the wrestlers say. Nobody else but God knows anything worth remembering."

And J. L. climbed into bed, put his arms around both Tara Sue and Delta Ray, and the three of them fell asleep like that.

Wild Sage

I sit here by my gate, sniffing the stalk of sage in my hand, and wonder about the leaves drifting down on me. They float past my eyes and settle on my folded legs. Summer green, pale yellow, autumn orange, cracked brown. But there aren't any trees by my gate.

A few Lombardy poplars protect the house, but they're a quarter mile behind me. Nothing grows out here except sage. I look up to see if memory has failed me, if maybe there's a tree I don't remember. Instead, I see something moving, something white penetrating the scatter of leaves. It keeps shifting.

The smell of sage is the only familiarity here. My husband's away, Russell just ran off to a friend's, and I'm trying to make peace with the letter from Canada that came this afternoon, the one that said my Jamie was getting weaker every day. My son Jamie. On a mission for the Lord. "He's wasting away," it said.

Jamie used to play in the hay rick with his brother Russell, jumping six bales at a time. I can't imagine him having anything but butter cheeks and bull's energy. But that letter said there's no color in his face, that his bones are sticking up under his skin. It said the Lethbridge doctors had tried everything.

It's not right, son. You're out there, supposed to be baptizing for

God. What's wrong? You aren't wasting away because of that girl, are you? You'd better be keeping your promise, Jamie. I kept mine. I didn't tell.

And more leaves drift onto my shoulders, covering my head, brushing my ears that are exposed because of the knot at the back of my head where my hair is tied up tight. I look up again to catch a glimpse of the white that is moving vaguely. The leaves fall thickly, impairing my sight.

When the letter came, I was rolling pie crust thin like a sheet of newspaper. The rural carrier usually finds his way to our kitchen and takes his time letting us know if there's a package or a letter. But today he must've smelled the sickness around the edges, because he didn't pull up a chair at the oak table or tease me into a piece of pie. He laid the letter on the table like a hot potato and hurried out the door. I dusted my hands on my apron towel and grabbed the envelope. I smelled something too.

Russell was shining mirrors on the toes of his Sunday shoes and laughing at his reflection—the chin man from the freak show. But he sensed something when I opened that letter. He stopped making faces into his spit-shine shoes.

"He's wasting away," I read out loud, "and there is nothing anybody can do. We've consulted doctors and prayed. He's too sick to put on a train for home."

My Jamie. Cheeks sinking into the jaw bones. Teeth poking out like a horseshoe stuck in his mouth.

"I better go get Dad," Russell said.

"Your father's too far away right now. Rode over to Cousin Lyman's to help with that caved-in roof. He won't be back until morning."

"He'd want to know."

"We'll have to handle this one, Russell. No time to ride for your dad. You don't remember when you were born looking like a dyed yellow chick. Royal was off doing the Lord's work, speaking at a stake conference over in Duchesne County, and you came early, all colored with jaundice. God listened to me then."

The rolling pin sat solitary on the thin sheet of dough. Russell and I, my hands covering both sides of his head, his face close to my bosom, started talking to God. We talked fast. Jamie was thousands of miles away. There wasn't much time with a week-old postmark and a letter that said, "He's wasting away." That's something I can't imagine because Jamie can run into the side of a barn and actually bounce, fly through the air and land standing up, like a big cat or something. He hops fences and runs through dry gullies like they're graded road.

Russell and I didn't squander time. "Lord," we said, "please. Jamie's good. This is a big mistake. You can't let him waste away. He's my son ("He's my brother," Russell said), and he's leaking his life out. Help him, we pray in Jesus' name, Amen."

Russell put his shoe shine rags away, and I headed for my bedroom. I closed the door, straightened the two crooked drawers in the bureau, and knelt at the edge of my bed. Rubbing the coolness of the rose satin comforter, I searched for my courage. I've avoided a little something with God, with my husband, Royal, too. It's about being a mother and maybe being foolish for my boy. But he's a fine one, that Jamie, good as they come. I raised him and polished him like the toes on Russell's Sunday shoes. Stroking the comforter, I sighed.

"Lord," I said, but I couldn't get my mind clear of Royal. Maybe I should've told him about his son. But he'd have filled with righteousness like a calf with frothy bloat and shouted that the law's the law. He'd have insisted that Jamie broke the law and must suffer the consequences. Royal would've kept his own son from his mission to Canada.

I'm sure I know my son's insides. I've watched him with orphaned birds, teaching them to fly. Nursing baby calves all night with an old bottle and nipple. I've seen him.

I saw him acting like a calf around that girl, too. Those loops of dizzy curls around her face and neck. He liked to put his finger at the end of each strand and wrap the hair tight to her scalp. He'd kiss her then. Something about that hair kept Jamie tied to that girl. His eyesight changed when she was around. I kept telling him, "Jamie, other things first. Forget that brown hair."

In the half light of my bedroom, I laid my cheek against the comforter and let the cool soak into my face. That big bed. Me and Royal under those covers. Lots of years. "Trust not to thine own understanding," Royal would say as he held me in his long arms while I'd try to analyze a problem. He'd pat my hair, my cheeks, tell me I was soft next to his body and fine as porcelain. "Let me and God take care of you," he'd say. Fine china for Royal.

I know Royal has soft places. I've felt them. But he's so stiff about life. Flesh clings to his bones like starch; he walks like his joints were made at a tinsmith's. He carries himself like his name, like a king. He wants things precise, not like me, believing in the soft side of God.

My knees tingled, reminding me of my purpose for going to my room. "Dear God, I know I'm just one of millions and zillions down here. I know there's lots to do in your position, but, just one thing—I know Jamie's worried about that girl, the one who tried to get a baby to keep him home, even if she wasn't successful. He said it only happened once, swore she guided his hands and everything else, too. I should've told Royal, probably the bishop too, but they don't know Jamie like I do. Jamie and me, we've been preparing for this mission his whole life. He promised he'd tear up her picture and spend every waking hour telling those Canadians what the Restored Gospel can do for them. He promised me about this, Lord."

And I felt Royal in that room, almost like he was hiding under the comforter, like he was trying to sit up and tell me not to trust in my own understanding. I smoothed the depressions of my elbows out of the comforter, no Royal, and puffed the pillows high and fat.

And the leaves swirl around my face like a small duster. One clings to my eyebrow like an eye patch as if to remind me I could be blinded by my first born and think he's a temple when he's only a whited sepulchre. And then I see a hand reaching through the veil of leaves, an arm covered in white.

All day I crimped the edges of pies and checked my bread for rising. I kept pulling that smell of new baked bread way deep into me, wishing good things all around my self, like maybe the Lord was listening. Then I'd remember the day Jamie said good-bye. He patted his shirt pocket. I knew her picture was inside. "You promised," I said.

"I'll do it, don't worry." He picked up Royal's best travel bag and settled it into the back of the buckboard. He smelled so good that day—like wild sage. We used to rub it on our hands when he was little and put our noses to our fingers. We'd rub it into our skin until we couldn't see any trace of the sage except for the grey-green it left on our hands.

All day long, through the dishwashing and curtain starching, I never stopped reassuring God that Jamie is on the level and wants to do everything he can to spread the gospel. He'll spread it like angel hair over the people in Lethbridge so they can't escape the truth.

"He said he'd repent so well he could look right into your face," I told God. "Like some of those Bible people couldn't."

And the leaves swirl, the myriad leaves and the intimations of white robes.

Russell came in from chores while the sun was dropping over the west fork.

"How are you feeling about things?" he asked me.

"I'm feeling strong as the smell of wild sage."

But then he looked into my eyes. "You look tired."

"I'm fine, Russell. Don't you worry about me."

"But I know your eyes."

"What do you know?"

"Troubles."

I wanted to pull my shawl around him and me and protect us from uneasy times. I wanted to spread my shawl out to Canada and Jamie. I'd walk across the plain, find my way to his side. I'd tell him to square his shoulders and rise up from his bed. He's a Mormon missionary.

"Baby child," I said to Russell, "I want to believe, but sometimes I'm a foolish woman."

"Don't call me your baby child. I'm almost as tall as you."

"I keep thinking you're still small, about the size where I can pick you up, keep you in my arms where there isn't anything to carry you away. Come here, Russell. Hug me." I reached out for my child who turned away, who kept just south of my finger tips.

"I'm going to get a breath." Russell ran out of the house.

"Don't you have a hug for your mother?" I called. He walked fast, moving his legs like he was racing with a train. Out the main gate, off down the road.

I followed him as far as the gate, and then I smelled that sage, right by the gate post, Jamie's and my bush of sage ever since he was a little boy. That's where we sat when we were talking about that girl. That's when he told me he was surprised by the power of loving a woman. Now my Russell was running away from me, too. So I stopped.

I sank into the dust, Indian style. I rubbed the sage between my palms, slowly, and felt the stalk break into minced pieces and slivers. Then it bunched together like dead skin rolled off my neck and gradually disappeared into a powder that covered my palms. I flattened my hands on my face and sniffed, trying to fill myself with sage, that dusty smell of Jamie and me together out there by the road, that talk about being powerful instruments for God. We made a pact. We shook hands, rubbed the powder against each other's palms, and we promised. As soon as this lie was over, we'd start again. Never, ever, would there be a breaking of this promise.

And that's when the leaves started to fall. While I sat in the dust by my gate, sniffing wild sage, these colored leaves drifted down around me, and now they're circling in the air though there's no wind and everything's still like after a snow storm.

Suddenly three men step through the veil of leaves and stand over me. I look up. They're dressed in white robes. They look like they've just shaved, and they glow like the vibrating heat of a mirage, their foreign-looking skin that's darker than mine. "Gather some sage," one says. "Send it to your son and tell him to make tea. He'll be all right."

Their faces seem to float above the collars of their robes. Their eyes are like stars spinning across the sky. I can see lots of time in there, time that I don't understand. Their eyes are full of pictures—planets, strange flowers, carved skins. Eyes like a mystery book, and I want to turn the pages myself, to read that book. And one of them has the leaves in his eyes. Every color from spring to autumn, changing as I look at him, and I want to ask how they change so fast, how there could be so many.

"Why did you come here?" I say instead.

"Because you love your son." The colors swirl, changing from new green to autumn soft lavender and back.

"I did wrong, didn't I?"

The eyes reel with winter snow and grey wind. They fill with the water and rocks of an Indian summer creek bed. Leaves drift onto the surface, their mirrored images darkening as they skim the stilled water.

He smiles. The leaves flutter up out of the man's eyes, some tangling with his dark hair. And before I can say anything, the three men disappear, following after a circular staircase of leaves.

When I realize they are gone, I search for footprints, but I can't find anything like a bare footprint, no rows of toes. I do find three leaves caught on the sage bush—green, lavender, and rust.

"They stood right by the gate," I tell Russell late that night when he creeps back home with the rising moon. "Sure as we're standing here in this kitchen. I brought back some sage."

And I rub the sage down to a rough texture and brush it into a white envelope. I watch that grey-green fall into the pocket of paper, and I make a little tent over my nose with my hands and sniff that sage as hard as I can.

Maybe Jamie did keep his promise, I think, tear up her picture and his feelings about that girl. Maybe he did put her out of his mind. Or maybe God can see Jamie's heart through my eyes.

Dear Jamie, I write, *Here is some sage. Make some tea and drink every drop. Everything'll be okay, son. You hear?*

The Boy and the Hand

Once upon a time lightning sawed the sky and cracks appeared in the roof of the day. About the same time, a family of four sat at the dinner table, huddled over their bread, corn, salad, and fish. The mother and father were arguing over minor points, as people who argue usually do.

"Why don't you turn the lights off at night?" she said.

"Let things be."

"Why is it you come home so late from work?" she said.

"Let things be, I said."

"Why can't you think of others, just once?"

"Why can't you stop saying why? I'm sick, sick, sick of why, why, why."

At this exact same time, the smallest child was looking a long trout in its dead eye. A trout browned in flour and salt lay lifeless and numb on his plate.

The young boy ate his corn and his salad of a few sliced tomatoes and pickled diced potatoes, but for some reason he couldn't touch the fish with his fork or his fingers or his knife. Too big. Too real, even with a coating of browned flour and crusted salt. The boy remembered other fish darting after minnows, leaping after blue bottle flies, racing in the shadows of the stream, and he sat glumly with a knife in one hand, a fork in the other, both balanced like small staves on the round oak table.

"Eat your supper," his mother said.

"I'm not hungry," the boy said, clenching his fork more tightly and wrinkling his lips, nose, and cheeks together in a toad-like face.

"Eat your supper," his father said in a solid, large voice.

The boy knew better than to say he wasn't hungry two times to two parents.

Without notice, the father's large hands reached over to the boy's plate and opened the fish as if it were a box with a hinged lid. He laid the trout flat and tore the skeleton right out of its belly. "Be glad your bones are stronger than this," he said as he piled the skeleton on top of the other skeletons on a plate in the middle of the table. "Eat your supper to keep them that way. Now."

"And why do you park the car in the driveway when it's safer in the garage?" the mother said.

"Are you going to keep this up?" the father said, two elbows on the table and two hands on his forehead.

"Why don't you answer me when I ask why?"

"I don't have to answer to anybody." Then, so quietly that the room suddenly turned still and the only noise was the storm outside, he said, "I'm not a slave."

"But ..." Most everyone's ears perked up—the husband's, the son's, the daughter's—when they heard a small "but" drop out of the mother's mouth.

"Yes?" the father said, his arms folded across his stomach and his fists tight as new buds.

Just at that moment the son stabbed his knife and fork into the fish and took a bite much bigger than his mouth. He stuffed the fish into one side, then the other side, and chewed quickly and fervently and obediently. With so much fish in his mouth and no chance to chew it sufficiently, he had no other choice but to gulp. And suddenly there was a bone lodged in his throat and he couldn't catch a breath and his father was flat-handedly hitting his back and his mother was telling him to put his arms up in the air to clear the windpipe and his sister was staring at him with wide eyes underneath electrified hair.

The boy felt as though he was being turned inside out, almost like the fingers on a glove when the glove is pulled off too quickly. The fish bone stopped all other motion around it. The boy didn't feel like a boy or a fish but something in between. He gasped for air until he turned red and the redness crossed his face and swelled his ears and burst. Everything softened to a numbing blue. He was a fish swimming under ice in a winter stream as the ice thickened and distorted and darkened.

As he felt himself sinking farther to the bottom of the cold stream, he saw a large hand—bigger than his father's hand, but not so large as to belong to a giant. It had no elbow or bicep or shoulder and floated across the dining room and over the table. It hovered over him—straight fingers like arrows, a thumb cocked like a rudder. It was a strong hand, not doubtful of its presence in the room. At first it was pale in color, like a distant star obscured by city light, but then it changed to green to pink to gray-black to pale again. The hand had geography in its palm—a map of the world, it seemed. It had sociology, the way it reached out and touched the boy, the way it vibrated ever so slightly and hummed.

All of a sudden, the boy felt the fingers of this hand open his lips and reach inside his mouth and grasp the tip of the fishbone and coax it from him. He felt his body rise slowly out of the stream, up over the water-smoothed pebbles and boulders, toward the sunlight and the reflection of green leaves on the surface.

"My baby," he heard his mother saying as she knelt over him, shaking him.

"Did you see that hand?" the sister asked. "The one that floated out the door just now with a fishbone between its fingers?"

"I saw it," the mother said as she held her son in her arms, rocking him as if she were a cradle herself. "And after it took the fishbone, it paused by my mouth, reached between my teeth and pulled all of the whys out of me. I don't have one left, not one." She tried to say "W ..." Her husband and children could read the shape of "W ..." on her lips, but they couldn't hear a sound.

"I saw the hand, too," the father said, his eyes like round coins. "And it shook one of its fingers at me as it sailed by.

The family returned to the dinner table. They ate their bread, corn, salad, and fish, they smiled, and they watched the rainbow arching across the evening sky through the glass of their dining room window.

That night the son and the daughter fingerpainted pictures of the hand to hang over their fireplace. That night the mother cross-stitched a sampler with a hand at the center of its design. The next day the father brought home a rubber hand from a costume shop and hung it in the kitchen with the pots and pans. At dinner the next night, they laughed about how foolish they had been and how lucky they were to have the hand come into their lives.

Peace reigned for a while, and they almost lived happily after. But before too long, it became apparent that mothers can ask questions without the word why; that fathers still don't like to be quizzed (even if they can laugh at themselves and hang a rubber hand in the kitchen); AND, even though eating might be easier otherwise, fish still have bones.

Devil Horse

On the road to the prophet's house, just after a buckboard passed and the driver tipped his hat, Jonathan's red-roan and broad-chested horse started kicking, snorting, and chasing itself in circles around its master.

"You, Abner!" Jonathan tried to hold the reins that had been pulled from his hand. "Stop!" But it seemed the horse had no ears. "Whoa!" Jonathan yelled, tightening his grip on the reins and pressing a hand to the horse's withers. Abner still bucked like a windstorm.

Jonathan dodged the horse's moves as best he could, given the burdensome weight he carried on his two feet. "Settle down, Abner. Twinkling of an eye, you're a crazy horse."

The horse jerked its head back and stretched its mouth into what looked like a cruel smile. The expression reminded Jonathan of a devil who'd take a man's soul away on a platter, no questions asked. Jamming his hands into his pork loin hips, Jonathan summoned every ounce of authority from every pound of his abundant flesh. "Stop. Now!" But shouting didn't faze the horse. It was spooked. It reared back on its hind legs again and tore at the air with its hooves. As Jonathan fumbled for a sugar cube in his pocket, Abner ripped the reins from him and raced like a fuse, a flaming red horse burning up the road to Nauvoo.

Jonathan examined the rope burn on his fleshy hands. Blood beaded on the wound. "What in the name of ... All I said was 'We're going back home!'" He looked at the road, then the sky. Buggies and three-seated wagons had bustled past all morning on their way to Friday's market. The day had been full of promise. Brightest of blue. But now, the edge of the sun was blurring and a faint curtain of clouds filtered the color from the sky. Suddenly, the road was empty, and this late autumn day seemed to move to a season of its own. Nobody's cargo creaked over the uneven ruts. The mud-hardened imprints of wheels and hooves seemed deeper than before. The trees seemed to be pulling away from the edge of the road, their branches lifting their leaves higher than they'd been, too high for shade. Even the sun moved to a more distant place.

He considered his choices: walk back to Scott County after he'd been riding most of yesterday and last night, more than a hundred miles, or follow the hard-baked road until he found Abner, his usually placid horse who was bound to outrun this strange venom sooner or later. Given the fact that Abner was the only horse he owned and the additional fact that Jonathan was not fond of walking, he turned toward Nauvoo.

His tender sides and hips still hadn't recovered from his too few hours of sleep by the side of the road where he'd curled into a ball of himself, thin blanket over his torso, cold seeping into his bones, and various critters touring the wrinkles of his worn suit and weary body. But before he'd walked too far, he shot a quick glance back over his shoulder at the face-down book by the side of the road—the one he'd tossed to the ground in the early morning light. He was glad it was in the dust where it belonged. He was glad it was a diminishing speck and glad the possibility of his being a too-easily-led fool for God was fading with every step forward.

"Too many curses in that book," he mumbled as he swung his satchel over his shoulder and whistled quietly in time to his steps—the only sound he could hear. Soon the whistling turned to humming, then to the singing of a song he'd heard only two days ago: "A poor wayfaring Man of grief, hath often crossed me on my way, who sued so humbly for relief that I could never answer nay."

The young man who'd sung that song had a voice as clear as spring water. He'd sung the same verse three times as he stood in front of the meager congregation at the old Methodist church in Winchester, Scott County, claiming to be a minister of God. Strange young man. Big Adam's apple. Hawkbeak nose. Jacket sleeves too short for his arms.

Jonathan remembered the feel of the church's door frame against his shoulder as he'd leaned farther outside than inside the building, trying not to be captivated by yet another dazed minister, yet another fool looking for God. Why were there so many and why was he still one of them? *Voice like my mother's crystal, though. Never heard anything like it, the way it rang through that one-room chapel.*

Suddenly, every muscle in Jonathan's neck tightened. *What was that sound? Footsteps?* He turned to see what, if anything, might be behind him, but he only saw the stretched-out bareness of the road. Except he'd never seen the road this lumpy before, or even the sky mixed up the way it was. The color had gone out of everything.

"A poor wayfaring Man of grief ..." He couldn't help but sing that haunting line again to the rhythm of his footsteps, even if he'd been hoodwinked by that pure voice sounding like an angel's. Young man, gawky as a scarecrow, making him lose his good sense and hold out his hand for a copy of the Book of Mormon. Jonathan Wilkins. He. Himself. A reasonable man who only wanted to find God.

That same Book of Mormon now cast aside at the edge of the road, hopefully far behind him by now. How could he have been so deluded? He'd been unable to put the book down the day before yesterday. He'd read it as he ate breakfast and told his wife he must go see the Mormon prophet before another minute ticked on the clock. But, this morning, after reading one too many curses on wrongdoers in the pale rose light of this particular morning—"names blotted out," "The Spirit of God doth not dwell in unholy temples"—his eagerness for the book and its message turned sour. All humans were unholy. Everyone sinned. So why the blotting out of names? The damnation? It was the old Arbitrary God again, and Jonathan had thought he'd found something better. He tossed the book just as the sun peered over the tops of the trees. "It's time to go home," he announced to Abner. Now his horse was gone. Frothed up and frog-eyed and scattered like the wind. And Jonathan was nowhere near home.

Is that the sound of my feet? He stopped abruptly to listen, turned around once again, but only saw a dust devil moving across the road.

Before turning back, though, he noticed something unusual about it—its shape, its movement, its hint of human form. Not enough sleep, he told himself, as he stubbed the thin sole of his shoe in the hardpan road. He whistled again to scatter his thoughts, then puffed his cheeks, held them big for as long as he could, and released the air with a burst. "Stupid arse of a horse," he exhaled as he straddled the deep trace of a wagon wheel, his legs wide apart and awkward, and looked for a smoother portion of road on which to walk.

"You'll never know the truth." The voice came from behind him, and Jonathan turned with a jerk. The man wore a black three-piece suit and his collar was stiffly starched and fastened with a maroon-colored cravat. His face seemed made of earthenware and his eyes jet black porcelain. A purple carnation was pinned to his lapel. A handkerchief was folded in the shape of a hexagon in his coat pocket. "You forgot your book."

The man held out the dusty, bruised book Jonathan had left by the roadside, and he smiled until it seemed Jonathan could see every tooth in his mouth. "Your teeth," Jonathan said, close to being speechless. "They're so white."

"They're not teeth, they're fangs," the man said, then laughed, throwing his head back with abandon. "I'm the serpent, here to guide you." When Jonathan didn't join in the laughter, the man said, "Forgive me. I feel the need for jesting today. I've been trailing behind you, and now I'm weary of traveling alone. I noticed you left a book by the road. Here. Joe Smith's Gold Bible, is it? Now, wouldn't old Joe like that, a devil like me delivering his Bible to a stranger!" The man laughed again, his laughter echoing in the emptiness of the road. Jonathan trembled as he felt the man's hot-to-the-touch hands place the book in his hands. The light of the day was becoming stranger than before, the trees taller, the sun colder and more diffuse.

"Something tells me," the man smiled, his dazzling white teeth brighter than anything else in the vicinity, "your horse is about a mile up the road, waiting for you. Rather wild one, I'd say. But then, you tossed this book away. What else could you expect?"

The book grew hot against the welts on Jonathan's hands. The road suddenly seemed a molten lava flow—unpredictable beneath his feet. The soles of his shoes felt as if they were melting. The road that had once been a sturdy, reliable road, was now a place where trees billowed like sails and fantastic bubbles of clouds swelled to the point of bursting. The stranger began marching, his steps high. "Hold that book," he shouted as he marched. "Witness for Christ. You'll be a god some day, they say. You'll build a better world." And then the man stopped and turned square to Jonathan with a slash of hot yellow in his eyes. "Drop that book again," he commanded. "Let me watch you this time as you curse it and throw it in the dust."

Jonathan had no muscles that could move. His fingers were paralyzed.

The stranger lifted his arm, pointed at Jonathan, and his outstretched hand turned to flame. Sweat lined up like pearls in the lines of Jonathan's face and neck. "Our Father, who art in heaven. Hallowed be ...," he whispered frantically as one of the overripe clouds burst and dropped a heavy mist around him, frigid as early winter morning on the river. It iced the soft hair on Jonathan's face and the tips of his nose and ears and eyelashes. He hunched inside his thin jacket for warmth, but there wasn't enough cloth for anything more than his portly chest, arms, and shoulders. He hugged himself, pressed his satchel to his chest, blew into his hands, but then, just as suddenly as it had fallen, the mist lifted. Jonathan felt the sun on his back, thawing him, telling him the world was once more what he knew it to be. He heard a bird chirping, saw a squirrel scampering across the road, and heard wheels squeaking over uneven ground. He looked cautiously to the sides and back of himself. He was alone, thank the heavens. Everything was the same as before, with one small exception: the book in his hand.

"Hey, Mister," someone yelled at him. Jonathan looked up as two men on high-spirited horses galloped toward him. "You by any chance owner of that heat lightning horse?" a yellow-haired man with a flat-brimmed hat said as he and his traveling companion reined their horses to a canter.

"Probably," Jonathan said in a dazed voice.

"Roan devil of a horse?"

"It could be Abner."

"I ain't never seen anything like it. Foaming at the mouth. What you been doing to that horse, Mister?"

"I just said I didn't like this book." Jonathan pointed to the battered book in his hand.

"For your information," the man said as he leaned to untangle his horse's mane, "your horse's grazing near the corner of a fence by the next turnoff. Some man in a black suit tried to tie him up, but the horse was impossible to catch—so many contortions, like it was trying to tie itself in a knot. But as soon as the man disappeared, the horse calmed down, dead still, as if nothing had happened." The two men pressed their knees into their horses' sides and galloped down the road. "Never saw the likes," the other man yelled over his shoulder.

"He's my only horse," Jonathan shouted after them.

First he walked one way, then another in the autumn sunlight while swirls of motes circled his head. He turned a slow, thorough turn to check the landscape for the man in the black suit. All he could see was a dusky raven flapping its wings, lifting off a fence post, soaring full-winged over the trees. All he could hear was the raven's throaty caw. And he felt his fingers curled tightly around the binding of the book.

Jonathan sighed and turned toward Nauvoo once again. As a cart loaded with green and yellow squash rolled over the baked clay of the road past him, he thought of the young man who'd preached in the Methodist chapel, singing the song that wouldn't leave his mind. The one who looked at him with eyes clear like a tunnel to a place Jonathan had always wanted to see, even if he knew better. A steady place where the weather didn't change. A place of harmony.

He noticed the fence posts, the crooks in the tree branches, the tall straw-like grass. Their wavy lines had changed back to straight ones, the distorted half circles in the vees of the trees transformed back to ordinary angles. In the distance, waiting patiently, stood his horse, Abner, his head drooping like a day lily when the sun goes down. Jonathan had never seen such a change in anything still alive. He eased up to Abner's side and slipped the bit and bridle in his mouth. Abner was docile as a sleeping lamb.

Jonathan finally arrived at the prophet's house, his face pasty with sun, sweat, and the dust of the road. As he stood on the front porch with the book in his hand, he suddenly felt overwhelmed by too few hours of sleep and too many hours of pounding the road with his short and unexercised legs. He lifted his tired hand to knock on the door, but then felt a red flush stinging his cheeks. *This man is called a Prophet of God.* Jonathan's face burned as he felt himself so close to foolish again. What could be worse than a fool for God standing on the doorstep of a man people say talks to God?

When the door opened, Jonathan gazed up at a tall man with the nose of a Roman statue and the eyes of the singer he'd met back in Winchester. Jonathan stepped over the threshold without thinking, as if he'd been invited in. But no words had been spoken.

"I've been expecting you," the prophet said.

Jonathan lifted his eyes and tipped his head back to speak. "You've been expecting me?"

"Strangers are welcome. Follow me." The prophet opened a narrow door in a narrow hall. "Dinner is at 6:00 o'clock. Rest. You've had a hard journey."

After dinner they sat in a small library crowded with books, stalwart faces in oval frames on the wall, and a fireplace.

"I want to know God," Jonathan said as he crossed his short legs at the ankles. "I can't help myself."

The prophet lit the kindling for the fire. "That is also my greatest desire."

"He nips the seat of my pants and nudges me, reminding me we're all sinners, every one. But can we mortals ever fathom a God with a frightening face?"

"The human mind can only see in small ways. Think rather of worlds within the universe, within the world of the stars and the moons and the sun. Think of the cornucopia of God, of the fruit, the issue, the abundance. Human eyes can never see far enough. We must build a new kingdom—a Kingdom of God, not the selfish kingdom of men."

Jonathan's eyes began to water and catch the light of the fire. "I want God to be something I can understand, but maybe that's not possible." And as he said those words, he began to hum the song again. When he realized what he was doing, he stopped abruptly.

The prophet unfolded his long arms and legs, rose from his chair, dug his hands in his pockets, and stood in thoughtful profile between Jonathan and the fire. His patrician nose was the same as one painted on a face on a canvas on the wall, his eyebrows wiry, one side of his face the moon, the other the sun. The prophet turned toward his visitor. "How do you know that song?" he asked.

"In Winchester. At a Methodist church. A missionary."

The prophet closed his eyes and began to sing the same song, not only one verse, but verse after verse. He sang of a man who met different strangers locked in prison and beaten by the side of the road. In the last verse one of the strangers stepped out of disguise. It was Jesus. "Of me thou hast not been ashamed," he said. When finished singing the last word of the song, the prophet stared at the world beyond the walls.

Jonathan pulled his body from his chair and stood as tall as he was able, his head reaching to the second button from the top on the prophet's shirt. "Your voice sounds like the young man who sang this song to me a few days ago. You could be brothers." Jonathan put his hands in the hands of the prophet. "I accept your God." The prophet squeezed Jonathan's hands and bent to embrace the round little man.

In the foggy, cold light of the morning, the two men rode their horses to the banks of the Mississippi where Jonathan's sins would be washed away. But as they dismounted and stood together on the bank near a bending willow, Jonathan's sense of beatification was jolted by a sharp breeze off the river.

"One thing bothers me," he said as he unlaced his shoes and placed them side by side on a soft bed of dew-covered leaves.

"Yes?"

"I'm here to be buried and rise anew from these waters, but answer one last question."

"Of course."

"Why ..." Jonathan's words halted behind his teeth.

"Go on," the prophet urged.

Jonathan cleared his throat as he removed his coat. "Why ..." He cleared his throat again. "Was it the Devil that brought me the Mormon Bible after I left it by the road and the Devil that possessed my horse yesterday?"

"You fear the Devil, do you?"

Jonathan took a step backward. "Doesn't everyone?"

"You must understand," the prophet said. "He has his unseemly methods, but he's still a son of God. Might he not work for God from time to time?"

"That's blasphemy," Jonathan said, trampling the tall grass with his heels as he backed farther away from the prophet, his body suddenly rigid as a bullet casing.

"Open your mind to the possibilities," the prophet said, reaching down to hold Jonathan's shoulders firmly. "I thought you, of all people, were opposed to an arbitrary God."

"But why was the Devil the one to put a sacred book back in my hands?"

The prophet lifted his chin and squinted at the ripples of the river capped by steel gray light. "Maybe he's a stranger in disguise," he said. "Yet another teacher."

Jonathan pulled at the hairs in his long sideburns and pulled Abner closer to his side and stroked his mane. He looked at a boat moving steadily through the gray mist and lifted his eyes to the overhead fog, which seemed to be moving steadily above him, not unlike the river. "Everything's possible, I guess."

"Everything," the prophet said.

Jonathan slowly unbuttoned his shirt, as if each button were a thought he pondered. He unbuttoned the cuffs and carefully slipped from his shirt. He unbuckled his belt and eased his pants to his feet. The rolls of his stomach fell free without his belt; his flesh sagged in tiers of tender pink. He wrapped a sheet he'd carried from the prophet's house around himself and mounted his horse.

"I put my hands in yours, but if it's all right with you, Abner and I want to be baptized at the same time. Yesterday was more than we'd care to repeat."

The prophet smiled, grinned, then slapped his knees and laughed. "You think you can be protected from God then?"

But Jonathan had already ridden Abner into a shallow eddy of the cold-running river and sat as tall as he could in the saddle, wrapped in a white sheet, waiting.

Ida's Sabbath

For the 1,039th Sunday, Ida sat at the church organ. As she played the prelude music, she peered over her reading glasses at the bishop's two counselors sitting on the speaker's stand, at their blue serge, gray pin stripes, and balding pates. Then she thought of the night before and blushed in places no one could see.

Quickly she flipped to a different page in *Quiet Music for the Church Organist* and played "In the Garden." Why did she keep using this book with its dog-eared pages? she wondered. Her fingers knew which keys to press. No thought. No sight reading necessary. Except for the three Sundays she'd missed due to emergencies, Ida had played the Gardenville Ward organ for twenty years. Almost. It would be exactly twenty years next Sunday.

The first absence, she'd sliced her finger chopping onions for a meat loaf and spent Sunday morning getting stitched back together. The second time, her daughter Raylene gave birth to a seven-pound girl. Because Raylene's husband Jody was crawling through a jungle somewhere in Viet Nam, Ida paced the hospital floor for both Jody and herself. Then there was Louis, Ida's ex-husband. She missed one Sunday because of him.

Except for today, Ida was always fifteen minutes early to sacrament meeting, sliding the hymn numbers into the slots on the gothic-shaped hymn board at 9:45 a.m. She always dressed in soft pastels because her friend, Milly, who learned about color coordination from her cousin in Salt Lake City, told her she was a "Spring" and looked best in soft greens, pinks, and blues. And she always played prelude music by 9:55. This morning she wore a tailored pink linen suit and posted the hymn numbers, but, like everyone else, she was twenty minutes late. Nobody had time to catch up on the week's news, pat babies' heads, or inquire about missionaries in Chile, New Jersey, and Taiwan who were out asking strangers if they wanted to know more about the Mormons. The world had turned last night, and nothing was the same. The atmosphere in the chapel was edgy.

It wasn't until 10:15, shortly after the power returned to Gardenville and there was finally electricity to run the organ, that Ida sat down to play the prelude music. And now, at 10:20, Bishop Jensen was climbing the speaker's stand. The pockets under his eyes were puffy, his hair looked like he'd been combing it with his fingers, and he didn't smile, say his usual "Hello, Sister Rossiter" to Ida, or walk over to the organ to shake her hand. He'd probably stayed up all night moving his sheep out of the storm, and now he was facing another uneasy flock.

Whatever the case, being ignored by the bishop flustered Ida. He was one of the few members of the congregation who recognized the Ida she knew she was—the woman who was vivid on the inside, a brighter essence than the pastels she wore. Maybe God had whispered in his ear early this morning and told him what she'd done behind closed blinds last night. She repeated "In the Garden," forgetting she'd already played it twice.

After a brief huddle with his counselors, Bishop Jensen walked to the pulpit. He shook out the creases in the knees of his trousers, tried to smooth his rust-brown hair that wouldn't be smoothed, and grasped both sides of the pulpit as if he needed them. Ida quickly found a resolution for the unfinished "In the Garden."

"Welcome, Brothers and Sisters," he said without his usual smile. "Welcome to another Sabbath, though the most unusual one I can remember. I'm sure you noticed our steeple, or what's left of it, as you came to church this morning ..."

Ida felt her neck muscles turning to steel cable and her vision filling with floating shapes, some of them resembling microscopic creatures of the water-world. She closed her eyes and pushed her fingers against her temples to keep a headache at bay. Behind her eyelids, however, the amoeba-like shapes swam faster. Ida thought of her temple garments still hanging damp on the shower rod and felt her naked skin against pink linen. She felt the absence of the shield of the Lord.

"... and Brothers and Sisters," Bishop Jensen continued, "it seems the Lord is testing our faith. With that in mind, let's open our hymn books to page 243 and sing 'Let Us All Press On,' after which Brother Bill Parsons will open our meeting with prayer."

She waited for him to announce her name, to say "Our opening hymn will be accompanied by Sister Ida Rossiter," but he just carried his notebook, face open, back to his seat, as if he were in a trance. The linen side seams of her skirt scratched her thighs and hips. She didn't have one pair of regular underpants to her name, never needing them until today. She squeezed her knees together, tighter than clam shells.

Suddenly she was aware of Morris Sant, the chorister, waiting, his arm half raised, for the introduction to the hymn. How long had he been standing there? Without waiting for his upbeat as she usually did, she pressed her fingers into the keyboard. The introduction and the first two lines, "Let us all press on in the wo-ork of the Lord, that when life is o'er we may ga-ain a reward," became a power struggle between Morris and Ida. She set a fast pace; Morris tried to slow her down; she raced; he glared. She played as if leading a charge; she leaned into the volume pedal on the chorus's "Fear nots." Morris finally looked at his hand as if asking why he needed one.

Her feet knew exactly which pedals to play without the assistance of her brain. During the second verse, her attention wandered out over the audience. All the colors people wore seemed tinted with a strange hue of purple, as though the lightning storm had left a fluorescent residue in the air. As her eyes brushed past Brother Bassett, sitting in the same place as usual and looking slightly purple himself, she saw he was staring at her, as always, and she quickly whipped her head back, eyes forward, to the organ, and squeezed her knees together again.

The nerve of that man. She added an extra trill to the melody line. *What does he want from me?* Even he would be surprised at Ida Rossiter, who meant music to the Gardenville Ward, a woman who personified dependability.

Maybe she didn't make dramatic entrances into the chapel like her best friend, Milly, Bishop Jensen's wife, who bought the latest styles at ZCMI's in Salt Lake City and who urged Ida to be more daring. Ida loved Milly and scoffed at the rumors that Milly once pinned up the sleeves of her temple garments so she could wear a sleeveless dress to a fundraiser for a state senator.

Maybe Ida wasn't especially daring. Louis, before he left, suggested she take some lessons from Milly to get a little spunk in her life. But she was loyal. She kept promises to God and her friends. "You're dependable as the seasons," ward members said, except Brother Bassett. He said off-the-wall things like, "You're a real sleeper, Ida. Pretty, too. No telling what would happen if your lid came off."

Ida didn't ask nor did she want to know what he meant when he talked like that. He was a renegade, slightly crazed since his wife died, even though it had been three years now. Ida avoided him both in the ward house on Sundays and during the week in the aisles of the IGA Supermarket.

"But the Lord," the congregation, finally coming together after the chaotic beginning of the hymn, sang the closing line rousingly: "... alone we will obey." Morris gave Ida the cut-off signal. She prolonged the swell of the final chord. Her fingers seemed glued to the keyboard and her feet to the pedals. The C major chord swelled and swelled until the organ was playing at full volume. The chapel filled with the power of music, as if, for one moment, Ida was playing in a cathedral with a vaulted ceiling—the kind she'd seen on the educational channel. The windows rattled. The flower arrangement quivered. When she finally withdrew her fingers and feet, she bowed her head quickly and folded her arms for the opening prayer as if nothing had happened. Morris snapped the hymn book shut and sat down, his face screwed with disgust.

Bill Parsons stood to pray. *Our Father, we thank thee for our many blessings.*

Ida's feet slipped off the organ bench railing. The extra gravity, maybe the devil, seemed to be pulling her pink pumps toward the big bass sound that would ruin the prayer and startle everyone in the congregation. She picked up both feet and hung them in mid-air, every inch of each leg clinging like a magnet to the other. Without her soft cotton garments encasing her thighs, her buttocks, her midriff, her shoulders, something in her was set adrift, something was loose.

And watch over all those who are not with us today, that they may be blessed and comforted. Brother Parsons prayed on.

Ida's glasses slid down her nose. Now her neck felt like six fused strands of steel cylinder. She wished this prayer would end and wished for the fiftieth time she hadn't put all her garments in the wash together.

Last night, for the first time since she married in the temple and accepted the wearing of garments night and day to remind her of her promises to God, she decided it didn't matter if she kept them off for a few minutes beyond her nightly bath. Just once. Just for the one hour it would take to wash and dry the pile of soiled clothes accumulated in her hamper.

After relaxing in her bath with two, rather than one, lavender oil beads, she decided she'd rather not step back into the not-quite-clean last pair of garments while she washed the rest. A complete stack of fresh garments in her dresser drawer would be such a nice gift to herself. A good clean start for the Sabbath. Stark naked, she gathered all the dirty clothes into her arms, walked through the living room, dining room and kitchen to the laundry room, and stuffed the clothes around the agitator arms. She added soap, liquid bleach, then turned the temperature selector to warm and the cycle selector to pre-soak.

As she stood in the yellow laundry room without any clothes in her arms or on her body, the fluorescent light purpled her forty-two-year-old skin to a frightful hue. Impulsively, she dashed away from the violet tones into the light of the white crystal chandelier over her dining table. She touched her thighs and rubbed her skin that felt brand new to her at that moment. It wasn't something she usually thought about. Skin. Her own skin. Suddenly she felt as though she were six years old, and she was glad she'd closed all of the blinds in the house before her bath. She ran through the house, turned on the stereo, danced to the German polka album her nephew had brought her from his mission in Germany. She danced until she had no breath left. She collapsed at the kitchen table in front of a long green onion and a glass of milk she'd set there before her bath. She was alone. What did it matter?

She felt the woven chair seat against the silk of her buttocks and the glass of cold milk in her hand. *What does it matter*, she kept asking herself as she nibbled the sweet onion. And when she returned the milk carton to the refrigerator, her breast brushed against the cold Kelvinator door and she stopped there, unable to move as she felt her surprised nipple grow hard and stiff.

At that exact moment the storm began. In earnest. After the loudest crack of lightning she'd ever heard, she stood helplessly in darkness, staring at the pyrotechnics dazzling even through closed blinds. Every time the sky lit up, Ida watched small roots of lightning working their way through the slits of the blinds as if they were searching to destroy. Ida, the sinner, stood naked in front of the refrigerator door, her nipples hard jewels. She fumbled her way into her bedroom and into her flannel nightgown to hide her nakedness, but bolt after bolt of lightning split the sky wide open, spread across the sky like the root system of a thousand-year-old tree.

Ida found a half candle in her dresser drawer, left there for times such as these, and a half-used book of matches from Zenna's Cafe, next to the dress shop where she worked five days a week. Sitting on the edge of the bed, she lit the candle and held it in both hands. She stared at its flickering light. Then she looked at the shifting shadows on the wall, Louis's laughing face among them.

"Ida's disobeyed," a voice that sounded like Louis said. Something that looked like his teeth shone in the candlelight. "Why couldn't you yield for me, you who like to think you're a sturdy oak tree?"

Next Brother Bassett's face popped into the shadows. "Your lid's coming off, Ida. I've been waiting."

"Get out of here. Both of you. In the name of Jesus Christ, just leave." She blew out the candle and threw herself on her knees at her bedside. She prayed until her cheek dropped onto a square of her log cabin quilt and her eyes closed and her hands unclenched. Still kneeling, embracing the edge of her bed, she slept.

In the morning Ida woke on her braided rug, stiff and cold in every joint. All she could hear was the sound of water dripping from the roofs and trees, still pouring steadily from the leaden gray sky. After shaking her hands and feet and doing a few knee bends to loosen her joints, she ran to the laundry room, tried the light switch, and discovered, to her dismay, that the power was still out. She pulled one pair of garments from the freezing cold water. She wrang the cotton as tight as it would be wrung, shook it like a rug, then ran through the house with it billowing over her head like a sail. After two laps through the kitchen and living room, she dropped onto the sofa. Her battery-powered clock said 9:30, fifteen minutes before she usually appeared at the ward house. Reluctantly, she slipped her bra, nylons, white rayon blouse, and pink suit over her naked body. She buckled the straps of her white high heels.

At the organ she felt her thighs sticking together like Scotch tape. They'd make a sound if she pulled them apart. Instead, she tightened her legs together. But that was even more uncomfortable. Too much perspiration, a steam plant, on the organ bench.

Ida turned her head toward the congregation. What were those people really like after they hung up their Sunday clothes? Did they ever touch their skin? And Ida wondered who had fancy lace underwear hidden away at the back of their lingerie drawers. Louis had always wanted her to buy some "just for special occasions." But she'd been faithful to the Lord, faithful to the promises she'd made within the holy walls of the temple. No frills for the faithful.

And bless our missionaries that the doors of the honest in heart might be opened to them. ...

When she saw Louis's face in the shadows last night, she thought about how he loved to slip her garments off her shoulder and kiss the tip of her left breast. She recalled the glow of his forbidden cigarette in the dark. Maybe she should have stopped nagging him about his tobacco.

Pretending her eyes were closed, Ida peeked at Brother Bassett and his wide-open eyes. He hadn't closed his eyes during the prayers since his wife died. He just stared and stared, even during the sacrament. Such a lonely man, who seemed even lonelier today. Deeper hollows in his face. Ida then checked out the Hatch boy and the Hall girl, who, as usual, couldn't keep their hands off each other. Ida craned her neck just slightly to see what it was they were touching, then caught sight of Milly Jensen in her red quilted Chinese jacket, glaring sit-down-or-die eyes at her climbing two-year-old who straddled the bench back, kicking the wood so everyone could hear.

Milly? How did she touch the back of her husband's head at night? Did she stroke upwards, feeling the short, newly cut hairs? Did she kiss the bristles? Watery shapes floated across Ida's vision again as she thought of Milly lying in bed without her garments, caressing her husband's neck and head, nibbling his ear.

After fifteen years of marriage, Louis stopped going to church with Ida, started to lose weight and smoke cigarettes again. In the beginning, he'd sworn off beer, coffee, and cigarettes, all for the love of Ida. But his new leaf had aged, crinkled, and disintegrated.

"Why do you have to smoke, Louis?" Ida cried for two days straight when she found out. "It violates your body. Your body is sacred."

For a while, in deference to Ida, Louis smoked behind the Lava Hot Springs billboard on the road out of town. He moved into the backyard until he said he didn't care what the neighbors said. Then he parked himself on the front porch in the evenings and smoked for everyone to see.

"We can't go to the temple anymore if you keep this up, Louis."

"I don't want to go to that sanctimonious booby hatch, Ida."

"Louis. This isn't like you. The devil has gotten his hook in you. Let's call the bishop."

"We aren't calling anybody, Ida. This is my home, and we're going to run it my way for a change, starting with you taking off those undergarments." He bought her a shopping bag full of pink and baby blue and lavender lacy underwear—her colors—but she'd hidden them in the basement, behind the bottled apricots. After he left her, she'd given them to Deseret Industries in a stapled, plain brown bag, double sealed with duct tape. She dropped them into the donor's bin in the middle of the night.

And bless Brother Nelson that he will be protected in his time of illness. ...

Ida wished the prayer weren't so long. She pinched her eyes tight to help her focus on Brother Parson's thoughtful words. Then she opened them just a hair to look at Morris, the music graduate who'd gone to the University of Utah and come back believing he knew more about church music than Ida. Still wet behind the ears. He might know about music theory, but he doesn't know the spirit like I do. He detests "The Holy City" and tells me not to use the vibrato. But she remembered rubbing her breasts ever so slightly against the Kelvinator. How could she criticize Morris after what she'd done?

And bless us that we may find the means to repair our steeple, and for these blessings we ask, in the name of Jesus Christ, our Savior. Amen.

Ida adjusted her slippery glasses with her right hand and pushed the diapason, dulciano, and 8' flute stops with her left. She tried to relax her legs into her work—the sacrament hymn: "There Is a Green Hill Far Away." But her fingers felt limp, incapable of the usual flourishes—scale passages, arpeggios, chromatics. Today, on her 1,039th Sunday, she could only think of that skeleton steeple, its shingles scattered over the roof and the lawn by God's own lightning. Her nakedness was rising like yeast inside her clothes, ready to burst out any minute.

She looked at her friend Milly, hoping she was looking up at her, sending reassurance with her doll-like eyes. But Milly and her blush-on cheeks seemed to be sinking in the middle of her five bouncing children.

Children, Ida thought. Raylene, she thought again. Raylene had little LuJean, but no one to help take care of her, just a dusty picture of Jody in his fatigues. Raylene, Ida sighed. She won't come out to church anymore. Won't pay any attention to herself either. Buys at least three of those chocolate-dipped cones at the Dairy Creme every night. My poor Raylene!

The congregation was singing the second verse of the sacrament hymn that Ida knew as well as she knew her name, when Ida heard the beating of drums in her mind—the snares, the two big bass drums of the Gardenville High School Band. She remembered the county-wide Memorial Day parade five years ago, the floats with the pretty girls, sun-tanned and moon-ripened. Opalescent smiles. Mascaraed winks. Mechanical waves to all the world from the Peach Day Queen and her court. Louis gazed after the float until it turned the corner. Ida perspired in the sun, wiping her forehead and neck with the handkerchief Raylene gave her for Mother's Day. She nudged Louis.

"Those pretty little things aren't for you, Louis. Keep your eyes to the front!" Louis looked at her as he never had before, with a watery stare and wire-drawn lips.

"I'm going," he said, his voice thinner than himself.

Ida's favorite band marched by. "Oh Louis, the Pocatello High School Band. You can't go yet." The twirling batons, the sequins and brass buttons, the drum major with the tall, furry hat low on his brow. Ida clapped with unbridled enthusiasm.

"Louis, don't you love it?"

"Louis?" She turned. She scanned the crowd, balloons, and sno-cone eaters. No Louis. No more Louis at all!

When Ida played the last line of the last verse for the fourth time, the backs of the patriarchal brethren changed to fronts, and everybody in the congregation turned to stare at Ida Rossiter, looking at her intently for the first time in years. Bishop Jensen leaned over to his first counselor, and Ida heard some words floating up to her and the organ. "Is something wrong with Sister Rossiter?"

Ida had enough presence to end the hymn with a resounding chord, pretending she'd done nothing wrong, bluffing as only a veteran like Ida could bluff, but her familiar surroundings were feeling strange and unreal.

The priests blessed the sacrament bread, as usual, and the deacons were passing it to the congregation in the square metal trays, but everything seemed off center to Ida. The floral arrangement sitting on the walnut baby grand, arranged and delivered by Bill Parson's Nursery every Sunday morning, seemed to be growing taller out of its wicker basket. The gladioluses' trumpet faces seemed to be opening and their stamens curling over the edge of the piano's top. Ida squinted at what looked like jungle-like vines. Struggling to meditate on the body of Christ, Ida nonetheless saw only herself in her mind's eye—dressed in a scanty pink leotard, her hair and nails sprouting wantonly. She was electrifying in all her pinkness. "Me Jane," she was shouting as she grabbed one of the vines.

The shock of her imagination brought Ida back to the present. The roots of her hair were tingling. She was blushing to her very bones and side-glancing at the congregation to see if anyone had any idea what was happening in her head. But her vision of herself would not be crushed, no matter what anyone else could see. It was like an insistent wind.

Now Ida was climbing the vine to the starspackled ceiling of the chapel. She scraped her fingernails across the rough surface and cleared a hole big enough to climb through. Squeezing through insulation, she picked her way through chunks of plaster and finally swayed on top of the church's peaked roof, clinging to the steeple's last timber. She leaned against the rough plank that had supported the steeple's copper, shingles, and paint for twenty years. She felt the wetness of the roof with her bare feet.

"You and me, steeple," she said. "We've been through a lot together these past years—you up here, a beacon for the house of the Lord, me below, playing the organ."

Ida jumped as thunder rumbled and lightning drilled the sky. She heard a voice next to her. "Ida?"

She didn't respond at first.

"Ida?"

She looked down at the hem of a fiery white robe.

"Tell me, Ida," he said, "what's going on with you?"

"Me? Well, I ... my garments, I mean, cleanliness is next to godliness. You know that. I was only trying to get my garments clean, and you know I've been good the rest of the time. I've only missed three Sundays ... "

"No man is good save God, Ida."

She thought of taking a direct look, but remembered Moses and the burning bush, about God being too holy for human eyes. The light was brighter than any she'd seen, even on this iron-gray day with clouds and a misty rain blocking out every inch of sunlight.

"Have you given up, Ida?"

Ida tried to pull her leotard down over her bare legs and arms, but there wasn't enough pink. She stood awkwardly, wondering if her nipples were showing through the flimsy material. Ordinarily, she would have shed tears of embarrassment, but Ida felt something else happening inside.

"I thought you'd be real proud of my twenty-year record, that is if you are who I think you are. Every Sunday when I thought about sleeping in, I said, 'No, Ida, forget your aches and serve God.' Now you're saying I've given up. When Louis left me, when I saw him once in town with one of the Peach Day princesses, even then I kept going."

"There's a realm the human mind can't fathom."

"Can *you* understand about Raylene?" Ida asked, jamming her fists into her waistline. "She was good as they come until Jody got blown to pieces in the army. And now she lives on Cokes and fries and too much ice cream, sits in the Dairy Creme parking lot every night, just waiting. She's my baby. My baby."

The last "baby" echoed through the streets of Gardenville, interspersed with rain drops, and fell to the grass. Ida turned and faced the blinding light, shielding her eyes with her hands but peeking through the slits of her fingers. "Little LuJean, too. She needs something more than a mother who sits and stares through a Chevy windshield every night after work."

"Depend not on thine own understanding, Sister Rossiter," the robed being said quietly before flashing up and away and off across the sky.

"Why not?" she yelled after the disappearing glow. "Why?" she yelled even louder, clenching her fists that turned purple, then white at the knuckles. "Why, why, why?" She stamped her feet and jumped up and down without remembering she was standing on the peaked roof of the Gardenville Ward in a leotard. As her feet slipped out from under her, she grabbed the lone timber of the steeple, hugging it tightly to her breast as if it were her best friend. She took three deep breaths. She looked boldly to the left, to the right, then pulled back her shoulders and head. She turned to the steeple and patted it tenderly. "We've survived," she said. "Barely, but we've survived."

When the deacon brought a tray of broken bread to Ida at the organ, he had to tap her on the shoulder to get her attention. She turned red as she looked up into his innocent eyes, sure that the young boy could read the moving pictures in her head. But this was the sacrament, after all, an expression of her devotion and her recommitment to Christ. She must calm herself. Stop this nonsense. She reached out and took a piece of the broken bread from the tray. She put it behind her teeth and closed her mouth without chewing. She let the sacrament rest on her tongue until it turned to liquid—the body and the blood—then swallowed it as if it were much larger than it was.

But then Ida realized she was sitting at the organ. She never stayed at the organ for the sacrament. Never. Always and forever, she moved over to a soft chair in an unobvious place behind the organ. What was she still doing here?

The enormity of her rashness hit Ida like a fist in the side of her head. It was one thing to dance through her living room singing "Beer Barrel Polka" and brush against door frames with her bare skin and touch refrigerators with the tip of her breast. She loved the feel of her body, free of belts and zippers and buttons and nylons, the feel of nothing between her and the air. A bird. Light and unafraid. But it was another thing entirely to have been presumptuous, even uppity, with a heavenly being, especially when she hadn't yet reached the twenty-year mark.

And, just as bad, Ida hadn't taken her seat for the sacrament. She'd stayed at the organ, sitting up in front of everyone like a sore thumb, forgetting her reverence for the holy. She was not in place. She was out of order, lost at sea. *Jesus, Savior, pilot me.*

When everyone's eyes were closed for the prayer on the water, Ida decided to make a move. She slid to the edge of the organ bench and stretched out over the chasm between the organ and the chair that was always hers during the sacrament and the sermons. She didn't want anyone to see her, but as she moved with her best stealth, she stretched a little farther than balance would allow. Her heel caught between two organ pedals, C and C#, to be exact, which everyone heard. Ida wobbled, tried to recoup, bumped her knee on the corner of the lower keyboard, totally lost her balance, and then plunged forward. Her head hit the wooden arm of the soft chair which should have been holding her safely on its cushion.

Ida's eyes opened. She saw the organist's bench above her and elongated bodies and faces peering down at her—the bishop, Morris Sant, and Brother Bassett.

"It looks like she's coming to," Milly said, kneeling over Ida, fluttering the air with a small fan.

"I knew something would happen," said Brother Bassett.

Ida stared at the blur of heads and shoulders and Milly's red jacket. She clutched the handkerchief that had been tucked neatly in her suit pocket. It was soaked with perspiration.

"First the steeple and now you, Sister Rossiter." Bishop Jensen played with the pearl tac in the middle of his paisley tie.

"Sweet Ida," said Milly, bending over and stroking her cheek. Ida could smell the lotion on Milly's smooth hand.

"I'm fine," said Ida in a wispy voice. "But isn't it time for a hymn, Milly ..."

"You stay right here." Milly looked up at the curious men above them. She pointed her finger at the podium. "You go put the meeting back together, Clarence. Morris, handle the music. I'll stay with Ida."

The circle of men dispersed slowly, leaving the two women together, Milly petting Ida's cheek.

"Milly," Ida whispered. "Are my thighs showing?"

"Don't talk now, Ida."

"But Milly, I'm naked. I didn't mean to be."

Milly dabbed Ida's forehead with her handkerchief and pulled the pink linen skirt back down over her thigh and her knee. "Just close your eyes. Don't worry your pretty head."

"But Milly, my garments. The washer ... the power."

"Ida, it's okay."

Suddenly, Morris was leading the congregation in an a capella hymn. "Milly, they're singing without me." Ida tried to sit up.

"You stop worrying," Milly said, holding her down.

Ida's face regained some color. Her lips changed from a pale blue to a faint raspberry as she looked up at Milly's thoughtful face.

"Ida, I've never told anyone, but," she lowered her eyebrows flat above her eyes as she bent close in to Ida, "I used to take my garments off once in a while. I liked real underwear on rare occasions." She whispered so softly into Ida's ear that Ida could barely hear the words. "But when Clarence got put in as bishop, he said I'd better wear my garments all the time like I promised. Our salvation, he said. But one day when I was about as down as a woman can get, I dyed an old pair of garments purple to pull myself out of that deep funk. Five years and Clarence still hasn't forgotten."

"Oh, Milly!" Ida winced.

"That's the truth of it."

"Milly. I can't believe you did that."

But then Ida smiled weakly, thinking vaguely of the feel of her skin, the delirious moment when her cells sucked in the air all around her, when she wasn't enclosed in white cloth, when she could sing and dance in the skin that held her bones, muscles, and bodily fluids together, out of control for a brief moment in time. And Milly understood what that was like. Ida touched the inside of her friend's wrist and then the softness under her jaw bone. "Louis always hoped ...," she said to Milly, wanting to share his part in this unexpected intimacy.

Milly bent close to Ida's ear again. "I know, Ida. I understand. Shhh."

Ida recognized the song the congregation was singing. Page 240 in the hymnal. But she couldn't make out the words for some reason. All that mattered right now was the music. The flow of the music. Lying in Milly's arms near the foot of the organ bench, Ida hummed along when she could.

Dust to Dust

The morning promised no bright sun. No blue sky. Only dust from the desert's chalky red soil. "Lord in heaven," Rosebeth said to herself. She stared out the window, worried about her garden. She couldn't see what little was left of it, its struggling vines obscured by the blowing dust.

"How can I feed my children if this keeps up?" She folded her arms, dropped her head to think, and for a brief second filled an imaginary cornucopia with squash, tomatoes, onions, and grapes from the fertile earth of her mind. Then the picture disintegrated into a dusty blur.

Everything around her was filling with dust—the cracks and seams of her adobe house, the braided rug, the plates on the cupboard. Touching her face, she felt sand in the crevice of her nose. If this kept up, dust would soon fill her mouth, her eyes, her ears, and Rosebeth and her children would be buried just like Kenneth.

She closed her eyes and pressed her fingers to her lips.

Dust to dust, the Bible says. God made Adam out of dust. He breathed life into his nostrils.

Impulsively, she rushed to the only door of her house and cracked it slightly. "Kenneth, is that you blowing around out there?" she whispered. The storm was too fierce for her to wait for an answer, so she quickly pushed the door closed, unlaced and stepped out of her heavy shoes, and tiptoed back to the window where she felt the rush of air through the chinks. It lifted the hair on her arms.

Suddenly, she sensed movement. The storm's chaos was cloaking something out there. She bit the tip of her finger. "No harm, please Lord."

Rosebeth hurried to the bedroom to see if Chad and Peter were safe. Her boys were still tucked in their small bed and protected by sleep. She tiptoed back to Jessica curled around a crocheted pillow on the settee, one leg dangling over the cushion's edge. Tracing the upper curve of her daughter's lip, velvet as the roses she'd have grown if the hard clay outside could have nourished them, Rosebeth wished once again she hadn't left England. Why had she rushed to the State of Deseret for the Second Coming?

Then she hurried back to the window, just in time to witness a sudden break in the storm. "White horses!" she said too loudly, then closed her mouth with her hand. She mustn't wake the children. She strained to see through the mottled glass. Behind white horses bowing their heads against the wind, there was a golden carriage. But then dust blocked her line of sight again.

"There's no such thing as a coach and four in this part of the world," she muttered, nevertheless leaning against the sill and waiting for another lull in the storm.

So much dust filled the air outside that it truly *did* seem as if the decomposed dead were blowing about, waiting for God to breathe life back into their nostrils. *Dust to dust, the Bible said.* Maybe, Rosebeth thought, some of it might be her Kenneth, her dear, God-loving husband who'd spurred his horse into a thunderstorm when he should have been warm by the fireplace. Kenneth insisted on finding the two lambs. When the lightning hit, it pierced his shoulder, his saddle, his horse Midnight, and exploded a nearby juniper into flames. When Rosebeth saw the fire through the drizzling rain, she somehow knew that Kenneth and Midnight's spirits had flown to heaven. She found their empty bodies next to the saddle burned clean through with the shape of a jagged star.

The storm outside was thickening to an angry yellow. "What's out there?" She hugged her shoulders tightly and leaned one way, then another, hoping for a break where she could see something besides dust. "What now, God?" she said in a hard-edged whisper, as if too much had been asked of her.

Immediately, she pressed her hand against her mouth to catch her words before they ascended to heaven to offend God. Before she could retract anything, however, she felt the power already in the room. It burned through her like the shape of a burning star in her heart. She shivered, pulled her shawl from the back of her rocking chair, wrapped it around her gooseflesh, and returned to the window to keep vigil.

"Kenneth was a good man," she whispered much more quietly, as if to apologize. "He loved us. He was scripture, the one that says, 'A merry heart doeth good like unto medicine.' If you are love, God, like they say, then you don't need him up there with you. You could breathe life back into his nostrils if you wanted."

Unreal as a painting, the dust in the window frame darkened to a deep orange as the wind churned the painted desert. Rosebeth stared through the window as if seeing nothing and everything at the same time.

What if this storm *was* Kenneth tiring of the Celestial Kingdom and impatient for her love? Maybe he was being sieved through the window in particles, a little bit at a time. Back to say, "Hello, Rosebeth. I miss you. I love you." Back to take her in his arms and whirl her in a fancy waltz as he used to do after a hard day of work.

"Daddy," Jessica said from the depths of her sleep.

"Don't wake yet, child."

Jessica stretched her arms overhead as if she were ready to wake, then tucked them back into her chest. Rosebeth sighed relief. She wanted to know what was outside before she answered anyone's questions. She wanted one clean look at the road.

And suddenly, there it was—a large gap of blue sky. In it she saw a coachman with gold braid on his sleeves, two golden post lamps, gold-leaf carving on the high sides of the carriage, and gold ornaments on the horses' reins. As the returning dust obliterated her brief glimpse, she thought of something she hadn't remembered in a long time. She rushed to her desk, pushed its roll top back, and pulled out her sewing basket. Lifting the lid, she pressed her fingers against the place in the lining where her own gold was hidden. When she touched the fabric, its coldness and unearthly smoothness made her remember that this was a piece of the same satin that lined Kenneth's coffin. Rosebeth had coaxed a yard of it from the undertaker's assistant.

The night before Kenneth was buried, she stroked this same cloth, trying to feel something for that stranger in that box who was so unlike the man she'd known, so immaculately still and immovable. Rubbing the fabric between her fingers, she'd kissed his forehead and closed the lid.

After the funeral, when her friends left for home, she used the satin to line her sewing basket. She'd sewn a gold coin inside, the one her father gave her when she set sail for America. This piece of precious metal meant she had something between herself and nothing.

She pushed the basket back to the dark corner of the desk, closed the roll-top, and hurried back to the window where she gathered folds of muslin curtains between her fingers. The door of the carriage seemed to be opening, unsteady against the force of the wind. She thought she could see the shape of one long black boot hesitating at the footrest, another touching the ground, a tall man standing in the road.

At first, he seemed in no hurry. Then he walked directly toward her door. Rosebeth held her breath and waited for his knock, though she wasn't sure she wanted to hear one. Was this a ghost? A messenger from God? What else could it be? Then she heard knuckles against wood. Five raps. Slowly, as if the air were lead, she opened the door a half inch and peeked at the man on the other side.

He was tall with a narrow, long nose. His face seemed made of ageless skin supported by the finest bones. Rosebeth could only stare through the narrow crack, her lips slightly parted. He wore white breeches, a blue velvet, long coat, satin ruffles under his chin, a barrister's wig—all coated with a thin red powder from the storm. He held a white lily, his right hand protecting its petals. "I come as your servant," the man said, bowing slightly.

Rosebeth shuddered, remembering the last time she'd seen a lily—at Kenneth's funeral. She scrutinized the man's slightly gray fingers wrapped around the lily's stem, and his face, which seemed neither young nor old.

"Don't be afraid!" The man put out his hand to stay the door. "Savor the things of God, not of men, Rosebeth. It's time for you to trust."

Rosebeth blanched at the sound of her name.

The man withdrew a lace handkerchief from his sleeve and covered his nose. Although his eyes watered from the irritating dust, he maintained an elegant posture and tried to protect the lily against the concave posture of his chest.

"People have told me," he said confidentially to the thin slice of Rosebeth's face, "a camel can go through the eye of a needle more easily than a rich man can enter God's kingdom. But few understand the words rich and poor. Few understand poverty as the condition of being without faith."

The storm blew crazily at his back, anxious to invade the house. "May I come in?" His words were muffled by the handkerchief.

"Well," she slid her fingers down the side of the door, "I don't think it's a good idea." She felt the bite of the sand on her cheeks and eyelids. "But then," she opened the door, "it would be unkind to leave you in this storm."

As he crossed the threshold, she became acutely aware of the way he carried his chest and head as if they were full of air. She wished one of her children were clinging to her leg so she'd have something tangible beneath her fingers to hold. When Rosebeth shut out the storm, his presence seemed to grow larger and wider and fill the entire room up to the ceiling and out to the walls.

"Would you like a drink of water?" she whispered as they stood awkwardly by the door. Without thinking, she fingered the collar of her dress where she'd embroidered her name in white thread. The night after Kenneth died, she sewed the letters to remember her name, who she was. No England. No husband. "I'm whispering because my children are sleeping."

"Water would please me greatly," he whispered back.

"I'd offer you a soft place to sit, but my daughter Jessica's occupying the settee. Have my rocking chair."

"That won't be necessary, but water would soothe my parched throat. And please, take this." He handed her the sand-pitted flower.

"A lily," Rosebeth said. Her cheeks blossomed the rare red of an apricot. "This is for a funeral. Is someone else going to die?"

"What about the lilies of the field, Rosebeth?"

"Fine words for you to say." She felt a hard place growing in her throat past which she couldn't swallow. He'd spoken her name which he couldn't have known. "Excuse me," she said, pressing her lips tightly against each other to hide her emotion. She rummaged in the cupboard for her only vase and a tin cup.

Tipping the water bucket, she sank a long-handled dipper into the last few inches of water. She filled the vase and the cup, careful not to spill. She slid the lily into the fluted neck, turned the flower to a pleasing angle, and set it on the wood table. Then she handed the cup to the stranger. "How do you know my name?" she asked.

"I know many things." He drank to the bottom of the cup, handed it back to Rosebeth, and looked down at her with mournful eyes. Under his gaze, she became aware of her simple black and white checked dress that she'd made herself, and her hurriedly plaited hair. She leaned into the table's edge and folded her arms resolutely.

"How do you know my name?" A wisp of hair fell over her eyebrow. She pushed it away.

"Does it matter?"

"What are you doing in a remote place like this?"

"I've come to see you."

Rosebeth shifted her weight from one hip to the other. He smiled. "One shouldn't take oneself too seriously, even if you're all alone at the edge of the world. You're angry at God, aren't you?"

Rosebeth turned her head to the side. "What makes you think so?"

"As I said, I know many things."

"So what do you know if you know so much?"

"At this moment, I know there is music on the wind. Can you hear it? God is all around us." Rosebeth squinted her eyes and tried to hear something besides the storm.

"When all else fails, I listen for music," he said. "It's God's gentle breath, you know. Today, it's a Viennese waltz." His eyes changed from mournful to shining, as if a thousand candles reflected their light in them.

"A Viennese waltz?" She and Kenneth used to pretend they lived in a castle on windy nights when even the stars seemed as though they'd blow away. She smiled faintly, thinking of how she once fantasized Kenneth's mud-caked boots were shiny black, that Kenneth was a captain in the queen's cavalry. Her visions of brass buttons and shining black boots were interrupted, however, by the persistent thought of her gold coin hidden in the sewing box. It burned oddly, like fire in her mind.

"Who are you?" Rosebeth asked, almost harsh in her insistence.

"Why do you insist on knowing who I am?"

"But where are you from?" Her tone was suddenly demanding.

"That, too, is not important." He smiled again, such a disarming smile that Rosebeth blushed. She'd only seen the likes of this man in the water-colored pictures in her mother's handed-down storybook. Her mother wrapped it carefully and tucked it in Rosebeth's valise just before her daughter climbed the gangplank of the steamer in Bristol.

After the long days at sea and harsh days of bouncing on a buckboard wagon across the endless plains of America, Rosebeth would find a place to herself—a porthole or a stream or a tree. She'd unwrap the book carefully and open its pages as if they were made of silken spider threads. In the fading light of day, she turned to each delicate painting and listened for her mother's voice: "This is for your dreams, my precious Rose."

But the manners of the storybook character standing in her house were alien, especially the way he swept his fingers through the air as if they were a fan in the act of closing. He was different from her humble Kenneth, who was so close to the earth. He seemed pinched in his chest and cheeks, an odd bird who, if he flew, would fly at a graceful tilt. And yet there was something about him that reminded her of something.

"Surely you can hear the waltz?" he said as he put his kerchief in his vest pocket. "May I?" Before she could protest, the gentleman's arm clasped her waist, his other arm reached for her hand, and he led her into dance. One-two-three, glide-two-three. Her cotton dress billowed as they whirled around the room to windblown strains of a waltz she couldn't hear.

Her better sense warned her to gather her wits. She was dancing in the morning when there were practical things to be done; she was only Rosebeth with an adobe house and a withering garden; she was in a stranger's arms. Suddenly, she was unable to lift her eyes any higher than the gathers of satin at his throat. She wished he would let her go, but his grip was firm.

One-two-three, he spun Rosebeth until she felt she would never stop spinning. She felt his closeness and smelled the traces of powder near his throat. For one small second, she relaxed and let herself spin with the assurance of his hand against her back. For a brief moment she felt her feet turn to wings and fly over the plank floor. One-two-three. She ventured a glimpse of his strong, straight nose, then the entirety of his face. She found his eyes looking back at her, staring long and hard into her soul. She felt them tunneling through her, back to the beginning of herself, back to the pre-existent Rosebeth. But then, he stopped.

"Trust not in the arm of flesh," he said, taking both her hands and pressing them to his lips.

Embarrassed by the sudden beginning and end of the dance, Rosebeth tried to find a place for her hands. One brushed her throat, then slid down to clasp the other hand. Shaking her head in confusion, she sat in the rocking chair and listened to the wind. Only the wind was real, her shriveling garden, her children who would wake any minute. She touched the dust on her cheeks again, fine as talcum. "Why are you here?"

"You must embark on a journey of faith with me," the stranger said, dropping his head forward in what seemed like humility, Rosebeth wasn't sure. "I've come upon hard times, I could say." Then he looked up. His gaze was direct.

She swallowed, the image of the gold coin penetrating her thoughts again.

"'Do this unto the least of these, your servants,'" she heard him say. She struggled to hide her astonishment and to keep back the words ready to rush off her tongue: *You're in no way the least of anything! You're a man with a fine carriage and satin breeches.*

"Anything you have will help me." His eyes had no lack of dignity. "I come as a supplicant. I have nothing but my faith, which I've brought to you."

"But what about the horses and the ... "

"I own nothing," he said so firmly Rosebeth suddenly believed him. His eyes changed weather, now like a deep lake with the wind whipping its surface.

"I have nothing to give," she said, seeing the gold coin even more clearly in her mind. Its image throbbed as if it were part of her heartbeat.

"Nothing?" the man said, a slight look of curiosity in his eyes, as if he could read her mind and see the coin living inside her.

"Nothing I can spare," she said as she surveyed the room to see if her children were waking. If a child would only say, "I'm hungry, Mama," she could be strong and push the gold coin deep inside her thoughts instead of so close to the surface where the man could see.

"Humans possess nothing," he said. "Everything is a gift. Where is your faith in this bounty?"

"But what about my children?"

"'Whosoever shall lose his life for me, the same shall save it.'" His eyes shifted character again. He looked to her like Moses staring into the burning bush.

"But I'm alone."

"What shall you give to find your soul again?" He seemed taller than before, as if he spoke to her from a raised platform.

The gold coin seared the inside of her head. She put the flat of her hand to her forehead to see if she had a fever, but felt only the insistence of something wanting out. She knew she couldn't hide the coin from the man any longer.

As she walked across the braided rug, she thought of her safety. The food for hard times. But this was what the coin was for. This moment. She knew.

She lifted the lid on the desk and slowly pulled the sewing box into the weak morning light. She felt for the hard coin in its secret place underneath the lining and carefully pulled a thread until it snapped, unravelled, and the gold was in her hand. "Here," she said.

"You will be blessed," he said, the pinched quality leaving his cheeks, his breathing more relaxed. He slipped the coin into his handkerchief. "Because you have given from your want, God's face will shine on you." Smiling broadly, the man bowed to Rosebeth, bending one knee deeply, his hat brushing the floor. "A queen among women," he said and turned to open the door to the dust that swirled around his head, his ankles, his velvet coat.

As she watched, Rosebeth could barely see the man climb into the carriage, the coachman whip the horses, the post lamps shine in the dense storm. The sand stung her face and whipped her hair.

As she closed the door, she stepped into her work boots, laced them securely, and leaned against the wall. She rearranged her turbulent head of hair and pinned it away from her eyes. Her hand fell from her hair to her neck and rested on the collar of her black-and-white-checked dress.

Very slowly she became aware of the raised stitching on her collar, the embroidered letters. The white thread on the black-and-white-checked collar. Of course. That's how the man knew her name. He was no ghost or heavenly messenger.

Rosebeth, she cried inwardly. She slapped both hands on her cheeks to waken herself from this bad dream. With one of her heavy boots, she stamped the floor twice.

"What a fool!" Tears careened through the dust on her cheeks. "So easily taken by skewed chapter and verse and a silver tongue."

The dust in the room rose as Rosebeth's angry foot struck the floor, slowly settled back on her shoulders, her hair, her clothes. Everything was only dust. Nothing more. Nothing less. Why was she subject to her foolish hopes when she should just accept that dust was dust?

"Mama," Jessica sat up and stretched like a cat after a long sleep. "What's wrong?"

"Your mother's a fool." Rosebeth paced back and forth, the boards sounding with her heavy step. "When we're close to starving, I give everything to the rich who get richer while the poor get poorer."

Jessica spread her arms like wings over the back of the settee as Rosebeth blotted the tears in her eyes with the heels of her hands. "Why has the Lord forsaken me, Jessica? Why don't I hear answers to my prayers?" She grabbed her daughter's hands too tightly, then sank to her knees and fell against the settee's cushion.

"I dreamt about Daddy," Jessica said, tucking her mother's hair over her ears and caressing her cheek. "He was walking in a field of white flowers. A bird sat on his shoulder. He was quoting scripture."

"What flowers are you talking about?"

"My dream," Jessica said.

"White flowers?" Rosebeth said, looking up sharply at Jessica's face. "Like that?" Rosebeth pointed to the lily in the vase, her voice unsteady.

"Don't look at me that way, Mother."

"Remember," Rosebeth begged. "Please try to remember." She dropped Jessica's hand, pushed herself to her feet, and plucked the flower from the vase. It was scarred, barely a lily. "Like this, Jessica?"

Jessica shrugged her shoulders as Rosebeth walked back across the braided oval rug with the flower in her hands. But suddenly Rosebeth didn't need an answer. She looked into the lily's face, at the scars on the surface, its long throat scattered with bits of dried stamen, the curling of the petals, the brittleness just before the crumbling. Rosebeth turned toward the door, reached out for the latch. "Listen to the wind," she said.

Jessica's face was a puzzle of confusion.

"Can't you hear him? He's in the dust." Rosebeth rolled the stem of the lily back and forth between her hands. There was a strange play of light in the door's crack.

"What, Mama?" Jessica said.

Rosebeth held the lily as if it were a prayer. "'They toil not, neither do they spin. Take no thought for the morrow.'" She opened the door and shouted into the wind. "I hear you. I hear you. I'll stop being angry or afraid, I promise you, Kenneth. I promise you, God."

As Rosebeth's last words died in the frame of the open doorway, the wind ceased. The storm that had been raging for hours stopped. For the first time all day, she saw the sun and the red hills against the bold blue sky. She ran out on the road to check for signs of the carriage. There were none. Dust covered any track ever made in front of her house—coyote, fox, horse, even carriage wheel.

As she gazed across the trackless sand, she clasped her hands and the flower tightly in front of her, so tight that the seed of faith trapped inside couldn't escape. The dusty vines of the garden rattled like gourds in the last gasp of wind, making music for this occasion.

The Fiddler and the Wolf

If only Old Dowdy had been quicker with his chores, he wouldn't be lost in this mucky fog and the twilight. But he'd dallied after milking his cow Hannah, hoping she'd talk back to him. He'd tickled her ear, fed her extra hay, even told tall tales, but all the cow said was "Feed me" and "Milk me" with the one sound that never failed her.

As he traipsed deeper into the less familiar territory beyond his fence line, Old Dowdy rehashed his theory that cows weren't as dumb as everyone said. They had cow wisdom, he insisted to his friends and his wife, Estrella. "Even the prophet," he told them, "gave a sermon saying animals had souls, just like humans." Dowdy wasn't just whistling up a crooked tree.

But, at this moment, he was lost in a porridge fog in his red and tightly buttoned lumberman's jacket, his brown knitted gloves, and his sheepskin-lined cap pulled down to his eyebrows. At this moment he regretted his theories about cows and everything else. Carrying his fiddle under his arm and wearing snowshoes made from strips of deer hide and steam-bent aspen, he started one way, then another, trying to find something familiar in the soupy fog. But snowdrifts and mist buried the road into town. Try as he might, he couldn't find his direction in the vast blanket of white turning blue in the last shadows of day. Everything was hazy and skewed.

After assessing the options, Dowdy decided he'd best follow the water. He could listen his way to Windpipe Spring, which was close to the south end of Doc Bell's pasture, then follow Turkey Gobbler Creek to town. That would be better than an invisible road leading nowhere. After all, the neighbors for miles around were waiting for him at Widener's brown barn, anxious to grab a partner and whirl across the straw-covered floor to Dowdy's lively music.

As his creaking snowshoes imprinted the virgin snow, he thought of the big barn swept clean and the plaid shirts and checkered dresses washed and ironed for tonight. He patted his violin case. It was wrapped in a special-order, sunset yellow blanket, which was his wife Estrella's Christmas present to his fiddle—Old Warbler. It protected Warbler from extreme changes in temperature.

Humming a snippet of a fiddle tune as he found someone's fence line, he groped his way past snapping branches and barely visible tree trunks. Dowdy could almost hear toes tapping in anticipation of his arrival. Everyone would be waiting for the breathtaking moment when he'd burst through the barn door. "Dowdy's here," they'd shout. Their feet would be itching while he opened his case and tuned his strings. They'd fidget until he sparked the air with lightning bug music.

His rising spirit of anticipation sang so loudly inside of him, it half obscured eerie howling in the distance. Dowdy almost took a fright, but then dismissed the thought. The sound was only music of the night. Music everywhere. "Ah-ooo," he howled back. A clump of snow fell from a high branch and caked his cap and nose and the red-and-black-checked shoulders of his jacket. He laughed like an old geezer, which he wasn't far from being. But then he reminded himself that sixty-two was still spry and respectable.

"Ladies to the center, gents promenade," he sang out as he tried to read his way through the fog with the outstretched tips of his fingers. "If you get a little thirsty, drink lemonade. Kiss your partner, the next lady swing. Left hand around the purty little thing. Ah-ooo, ah-ooo," he howled joyously at the echoing night. Everybody'd be dancing and whooping it up as soon as Old Dowdy arrived at the barn. It was Saturday night.

"There it is," he shouted when he heard the sound of water bubbling up out of the ground. "Windpipe Spring. I'm on course!" Now he knew for sure where he was, and, with a little luck, he could make it to the dance in forty minutes' time, maybe less, not overly late.

As if to witness Dowdy's joy, the fog separated. Dowdy could see the moon sitting between clouds like a thin old lady in a rocking chair. She didn't rock; she just leaned back dreaming an old time dream. The knot of clouds that covered her up all too quickly probably meant more snow, but Dowdy humbugged the thought and listened for the spring's stream which should lead him to Turkey Gobbler. Most of the water was hostage in clumps of blue ice, but there was a sliver of stream under the frozen surface that told Dowdy which way to go.

Then he heard the howling again. This time it was closer, just across the water in a cluster of pine trees whose tops jutted like arrows into the blue-black sky. Beneath the coat of new snow, the trees' dark branches floated over the forest's secrets, especially over the night creatures creeping closer to Dowdy.

"We drink lemonade and a little root beer," Dowdy sang another verse. "Sons and daughters of the pioneer." This time, though, he sang more softly. The howling was coming from not one, but from a pack. They were giving Dowdy fair warning, it seemed.

Ordinarily, he might have tried to strike up a conversation or leave a few crumbs of bread behind him, knowing wolves weren't interested in his sour human flesh. But tonight Dowdy was one and they were many. He had no bread, and he knew about deep snow and hunger. After months of winter, even chicken-bone, lean, lank Dowdy himself might taste good. He'd best find a place to make himself scarce. But, as the stubborn fog covered his path again, every tree looked the same, every branch pointed in opposing directions, and the running water seemed only an imagined sound in Dowdy's ears. He raised his eyes to the sky. "You there, God? Just in case, I want to say thanks for Old Warbler and music and Estrella. And, if you see fit, I wouldn't mind playing at the barn dance tonight. Hope that isn't too much to ask. Amen."

The very moment he said "Amen," Dowdy heard the rush of the spring as it joined with Turkey Gobbler right in front of his eyes, almost as if a guardian angel had moved it there like a stage prop. He closed his eyes and nodded yes to God. Yes and thank you. He could follow this stream to the old McCune place, given over to mice and rat nests. Last summer when he was tracking a lost cow, Dowdy explored the empty house and marveled at the cupboards once trim. Their doors were warped and hanging from single hinges; their insides were stuffed with brown leaves, nests, torn rags and papers picked up from who-knew-where by who-knew-who.

After working his way through a tight stand of trees and untangling limbs of a riverbush from the lacing on his snowshoes, Dowdy saw the old house looming large in the moon's light. The fog was behind him now, and he could see that much of the house's wooden siding had split; the porches had given way to the weight of too many winters; piles of snow curved high into the cabin's sides and sloped to the windowsills. As Dowdy came closer, he saw glittering swordtips of broken glass and a jagged hole where the window should have been. He'd been counting on a safe place. His heart sank.

Dowdy unlaced his snowshoes, stretched his legs over the porch's broken boards, and hoisted himself up to the front door ledge. The door was barely a door anymore and yielded easily to his touch, for which he was thankful. The wolves weren't far behind.

He looked for something to cover the broken window, but then noticed that the window on the opposite side of the room had no pane at all. Carefully, he rested his fiddle case on the floor covered with pine needles and dead leaves, and peered out first the paneless window, then the other. The snow sloping up against the house made an easy access for the wolves now at the edge of the clearing, though they seemed temporarily confused by the moonlight on the shattered glass.

Frantically Dowdy searched the room: the rotting stairway to the loft would be of no use; the wolves could climb stairs. He couldn't hide in the closet; one of its door planks had crashed to the floor. Then he looked at the only sturdy part of the cabin—a massive mantle built of waterworn boulders.

Quickly, he took off his gloves, crushed them in his coat pockets, and crawled over the charred hearthstones. The uneven stones jabbed into his knees as he crawled. Inside the narrower-than-he-expected chimney, he gazed up at the blackened stones and the spot of sky above. He sat up against the walls to see if he could fit, then remembered he'd forgotten Old Warbler. He couldn't play for the dance that night without his fiddle. He couldn't leave his best friend in a cold, empty house.

Crawling out from the chimney, Dowdy saw that the red squares of his coat were mostly black already—soot-covered, dark as dead and buried leaves. Leaving a trail of black handprints on the hearthstones, he quickly snatched his fiddle case. But the yellow blanket snagged on a splinter and pulled away from the rope securing the case. When he tried to fit it back in place with his blackened hands, Dowdy felt a pang of regret. Estrella was so proud of Old Warbler's blanket. But then he looked up and saw the heads of three wolves peering through the jagged glass.

Dowdy's fingers seemed like toes as he tried to tie the blanket back in place. Each time he took a fast look at the window, he imagined the wolves' fangs growing longer over the leathery curve of their lips. Finally securing the blanket, he realized it was only a matter of moments before the rest of the wolves discovered the easy way in. He crawled back over the hearthstones, his knees bruised from the first trip across, then hunched inside the chimney. He pulled his knees tight into his chest, placed his feet on one wall, rested the fiddle case on his lap, leveraged his back against the opposite wall, and inched up the layers of sooty bricks.

The fine powder of black carbon almost choked him as he climbed toward the oblong of sky where the rocking-chair-woman moon still tilted backwards. She languished in her eternal rocking while Dowdy battled with all his strength. She seemed so calm while, in the skinny, tight chimney, Dowdy's calves and thighs cramped with fierce spasms. Every time he stopped climbing to ease the pain, he had greater doubts about making it to the top. His knees and ankles and shoulders were shaking. But he had no choice. Finally, he wormed close enough to the top to slide his fiddle case to safety on the chimney's ledge. Then, groping for a handhold, he pulled himself onto his elbows, dragged the rest of his body over the capstones, and hung like an open jackknife. His breath vaporized the brisk air, and all he could hear was his own gasping.

After his chest stopped heaving, he pulled himself to a sitting position on top of the chimney. For a moment, Dowdy Kingsley, the old fiddler himself, was king of the mountain, enthroned above the pack of wolves circling below, all of them frustrated by Brother

Dowdy Kingsley.

Sooner than he would have liked, however, Dowdy realized his days as king of the mountain were numbered. The wolves were building a ladder up the side of the house—one standing still while the next climbed onto its back, then the next one climbing over them both. There were at least six wolves waiting for their turn to be a rung on the ladder. Never in his wildest dreams had Dowdy imagined wolves coming up with such a scheme.

Animals and music, he thought. He couldn't figure either one of them completely. A man could know about an animal's fur, its parts, or its habits, but he could only imagine what a human might do, not being privy to animal logic. And he might know about the notes on a page of music, but he never knew what made music talk or how a fiddle could capture the pulse of life with the stroke of a bow. These things were beyond knowing.

But the stack of hungry wolves was growing taller, and Dowdy decided he'd better stop philosophizing and do some quick thinking. This could be the end of Dowdy Kingsley, he suddenly realized.

What about Estrella, though, the little star of his life, the one who held him in her arms and sang him to sleep, his patient helpmate who never had been able to bear a child? She wouldn't have anybody to fuss over if the wolves got Dowdy. He imagined Estrella coming to him one last time with a bowl of steaming soup in her hands, dancing across the snow to his music, jumping weightlessly to the chimney top. "Oh, Dowd," he thought he might hear her whispering in his ear. "You play like the stars sing in the heavens because they're so happy to be near our Lord." Music. God. Estrella. All the same to him.

Suddenly, he felt the brush of something like an angel wing near his face and then some powerful force pulling on his wrists. Something was making him reach for his fiddle. He untied the first rope around the blanket. Then the second and third. The very smudged blanket fell open. His fiddle case. Dowdy unfolded the blanket and put it around his shoulders, black handprints and all. He unlatched his case. There it was—its worn scroll and fingerboard, its rounded belly and curved ribs. With affection, he traced the F-hole with his near-blue finger, then lifted the fiddle from the case.

With his chilled, blackened fingers, Dowdy adjusted the pegs.

They were tight in this cold, but Dowdy had a practiced hand that could find the right pitch without any hesitation. He played two strings together, finessed them into perfect fifths, and then droned the A against the other strings. "Ladies to the center, gents promenade," he sang as he prepared to play for God, Estrella, and the animals nearing the eaves of the house.

And then the moment of truth faced him as the wolf at the top of the living ladder peered over the roof's edge, sniffing, its pale eyes riveted on Dowdy's. At first Dowdy was petrified by those orbs staring him down as if they were looking for signs of weakness in his character. But Dowdy had his fiddle. He squeezed it under his chin and neck and began his favorite lullaby. He stared back into the wolf's eyes that seemed to have a flickering light inside. If this wolf had a soul, could it recognize his?

"Lullaby and good night" filled the air. The fiddler's and the wolf's eyes locked and became a circle like the moon when it was full. My life for yours; yours for mine. Which one?

The wolf sniffed Dowdy again and crouched low on its haunches. It stretched its neck until Dowdy could see faint speckles in its eyes and an empty, lean look near the jawline. The wolf licked its teeth with a pale tongue and took another step toward him.

Not flinching, Dowdy played boldly, even though his cold and nervous fingers struggled for a pure tone. His whole soul joined with the lullaby he'd heard his mother sing so many times.

Each hair on its body alert, the animal seemed aware of Dowdy's every move—the curve of his hand above the bow and the bow gliding between the bridge and the fingerboard. Above the intense eyes, the wolf's ears stood tall as if they could catch all things about Dowdy and his music. And the fiddler could feel the warm moisture of the wolf's breath as it spiralled into the cold night. He felt it on a tender part of his neck, just above his wool scarf.

As he reached the last notes of the lullaby, the part where he could remember his mother's voice singing "They will guard thee from harm, Thou shalt wake in my arms," the wolf suddenly lifted its head and bared its throat.

Dowdy could feel the hunger in the wolf's belly. He felt the deepness of the snow and the way an animal's legs sank when it tried to run after prey. He recognized something in the wolf like the water breaking from the ice in spring, something like ripe wheat blowing in wide fields, something like the sound of his fiddle. For one brief moment, he thought, "Why shouldn't that wolf eat me?" But then he thought of Estrella all alone and the people waiting for him at Widener's barn, lots of people waiting to drop their troubles and ease their cares and find new reasons to live because their dancing feet could carry them through another week of hard work.

As the last note of the lullaby faded away to a vibrating string, the wolf's ears perked up taller and straighter and it looked up at the stars. Suddenly its ears seemed as though they were nets catching the silvered fishes of a larger melody. Dowdy tilted his head backward and listened as he'd never listened before. He could hear the tops of the trees bending and the crisp air crackling and the ice crystals dancing through the sky. And then he heard a sound he'd never heard before—almost as if it came from the aurora borealis and places beyond the stars. Maybe the vibration of his last note had started a vibration up there. He and the wolf searched the sky, their mouths open, until silence returned and draped over them like a cloak.

The wolf looked at Dowdy. Dowdy looked at the wolf, whose eyes glittered with starlight instead of hunger. Before Dowdy could lift his bow to play another tune, the wolf backed away. Carefully. Respectfully, its black-tipped tail the last thing Dowdy saw as it sprang from the backs of the other wolves and leaped to the ground. The pack followed and scattered through the dark trunks of tall trees stark against the white snow and the moonlight.

Dowdy sat on the chimney for a minute or two, astounded at the turn of fortune, pondering the music he'd just heard. But time was growing short. He wriggled his icy fingers back into his gloves and tucked the ends of his wool scarf back into his coat. Then he slid off the tin roof into a deep bank of soft snow, re-wrapped his violin case, laced up his snowshoes, and followed Turkey Gobbler to the barn on Widener's place.

As he slogged the last quarter-mile, he decided he'd play his fiddle for Hannah as soon as he got back home. Why hadn't he thought of it before? Maybe then they could listen to the other music together, and she'd let him in on some secret known only to cows.

Lullaby and good night
With roses bedight
With lilies bespread
Is baby's wee bed.
Lay thee down now and rest
May thy slumber be blest.

Lullaby and good night
Thy mother's delight.
Bright angels around
My darling shall stand
They will guard thee from harm
Thou shalt wake in my arms.

Bread for Gunnar

No one seemed to know the man. His name was Gunnar Swenson, but that's all most people knew. He lived on the corner in a small gabled house with chimneys on both ends. Who knows how long he'd been there before my husband, Heber, me, and our four children moved next door.

We'd returned to the city, discouraged by the red clay country to the south. We tried to help build the kingdom for Brigham Young and the Lord, but Indians and scorching sun didn't want us anywhere near the Colorado—the big, unpredictable, muddy, red river. Gunnar didn't want us around either, it seemed. Whenever I was out in my yard, he'd never turn his head in my direction.

"Hello," I shouted several times, leaning against his fence and shading my eyes with a neighborly hand. "Hello, there," but he never paid a mind to me. Nor to the carriages and horses passing our houses.

One morning while I washed the breakfast dishes, I put my nose close to the window glass to watch him more particularly. He dug the soil, turned it over and over again, raked it, refined it, all for no apparent reason. After preparing the soil finer than powder, he never grew anything—no sweet peas, green peas, parsley, or thyme.

This reminded me of Call's Landing, the place we'd tried to make a harbor for river boats from the Pacific, the place where nothing had grown—not our crops, not our sketchy apricot trees. Heber tried to hide his disappointment in our communal and personal failure, but I think he was annoyed I wasn't the stalwart woman he thought I was in the beginning. "Heber," I pleaded, "I'm choking to death in this place. Take me back to irrigation ditches and some real mountains. I hate this bleached soil, creeks that run dry when the rain stops, and this arbitrary river that smashes boats to shingles."

I begged until Heber had no other choice.

"We failed the Lord," he reminded me the day we stuffed every crevice of our already overloaded wagon. "If I didn't love you and the children, I'd stay and finish the work."

"I'll make it up to you," I promised.

For just one brief moment, in the middle of his trying to understand me, he looked as if he wished he could wash me from his skin. He stared at me with coal eyes. "God would give you strength if you'd let him," he said, and then swept the floor harshly. For a brief second, I felt it was me he was sweeping out of the house. He needed a hardier woman, a partner to strive with him and help him find approval in God's eyes. But why think of that now?

Pulling away from the window and back to my chores, I scratched the hardened yolk from a plate with my fingernail. Then I looked at Gunnar, bent on one knee, the soil falling from his fingers. I leaned closer to the glass. He was exceptionally tall, stoop-shouldered, massive, and blond. Maybe he'd been a farmer in the old country who'd lost his property in a drought and converted to Mormonism to answer for his losses. Maybe he was a descendant of a North Sea Viking with no faith in the land. To see him sift the fine soil through his large fingers reminded me of the fairy tale giant who held small people in his hands, not understanding their smallness as they slipped through his fingers. I couldn't stop wondering about Gunnar's hollow husbandry.

On the following Sunday, as the weekly parade of Saints walked past our house on their way to Sunday school, my family and I joined the procession on the well-trampled path. As we passed Gunnar's front gate, I caught sight of him clipping individual leaves from a hedge with small scissors. "Wait a minute, Hebe," I said. "I'm inviting Brother Swenson to go with us."

Heber smiled as I lifted the latch, approving my impulse to tend to lost sheep. But as I pulled the gate open, I saw what moved like a shadow sliding out of view on the west side of the house. Sure it was Gunnar, I hesitated, dropped my hand, and peered into the shade at the edge of the house that now seemed absolutely still. Even the leaves on the vine had stopped rustling, as if collaborating in Gunnar's invisibility.

"Strange," I said as I turned back to Hebe, who was boosting Jonathan, one of our two-year-old twins, on his back for a ride. He took a few galloping steps, sang "Ride a Cock-Horse to Banbury Cross," laughed, then waited for me to catch up.

"I've heard Bishop Miller's been trying to get him out of that house and yard for a long time," Hebe said. "Nobody's had any luck, but if anybody could do it, you could. You're an angel. Most of the time, that is." Heber put his arm around my waist and nuzzled my cheek. I looked at my beloved, so close to me, struck by his beauty and by the intensity of his eyes and how his presence unhinged me.

"How long's Brother Swenson been in the valley?" I asked, brushing the unruly hair from Jonathan's eyes.

"Scandinavians been coming here in droves for fifteen years now. The bishop said something about a sweetheart died or maybe left Gunnar for someone else. Doesn't know for sure. Come on, we'll be late."

One August afternoon as I was fixing lunch with newly baked bread and preserved apricots, I watched Gunnar set his shovel, hoe, and rake against his house. Lifting a bucket from his porch and stuffing two paint brushes into his back pocket, he walked along his white picket fence to the public corner of the yard. There he squatted on his haunches and began to paint. Painstakingly, he pressed the brush against the wood until it fanned over the face of the picket and spread the most amazing shade of red I've ever seen—a wild sort of parrot red, a splotch of half-formed flying bird rising up out of Gunnar's yard. Picket after picket turned red until both sides of the front fence had no white to show.

Then, late that afternoon while I sat on my front porch with the twins and my mending, Gunnar walked out of his house holding a stack of calico strips in his hand. Keeping my face turned to my stitching and the boys, I watched him tie every other picket with a strip of calico, loop the material around the wood, and fasten it in a bow, as if his fence were some kind of valentine. In two days the entire fence bordering two streets, the alley, and our house was bright red and wrapped in calico.

"Heber," I said at dinner, my peas halfway to my mouth, "have you ever seen such oddness? Calico ribbons on a red fence?"

"I don't know how he stays alive or buys paint and ribbons." Heber dabbed his mouth with his napkin. "I guess the bishop drops a food basket off late at night once a week, and there are those who take pity on him in unpublished ways. Speaking of unpublished, I should tell you the stake president wants to talk to me tonight. I'll be gone a while."

"What does he want, Hebe?" My attempt at sounding calm failed. Heber's cheeks grew red, like Gunnar's fence. I saw my oldest daughter Elsie look up from her food, her ears alert.

"I'm not sure."

But we both knew. Lately, the stalwart men in the church were being asked to restore the work of Abraham—to build up the kingdom with more wives to father progeny as innumerable as stars, uncountable as sand by the sea. "You know he's been calling more of the brethren to live The Principle," I said under my breath because of my little pitcher with big ears sitting at the table next to me. "Elsie, finish your peas," I said too sharply.

"I don't want another wife in this family," I whispered, trying to keep my sudden anger intact, squeezing Heber's fingers until I could feel my fingernails sink into his flesh. Elsie kept her eyes down, but I knew she heard every word. "Do you hear me?" Heber shrugged and excused himself from the table.

"Only the best men get called for that. No need to worry about me."

I cleared the table, tucked Jonathan and Jethro into bed, read a story to Elsie and Liza, brushed my hair silky, and stretched out on top of the crocheted coverlet, a wedding gift from my mother. *Another wife? Oh God, please, don't ask that from me. Things are hard enough.* I tossed from side to side until my hair was tangled again.

I don't know how long it was before Heber tapped my shoulder and said, "Better wake up and get dressed for bed. You're freezing." His face was beaming down on mine as if lit by a piece of the sun. He was a handsome man, my Heber. He had a straight, strong nose, a broad back, a penchant for nobility. "The Principle," he said as I sat up, rubbing my eyes. "We've been chosen, Anna. Brigham Young has given his blessing." Heber was happier than since we'd been called to Call's Landing, glorying to know God still loved him.

"To me," he said as he patted my hip and settled into the mattress, "serving God is more important than my life! We're blessed, Anna. Doubly blessed."

The Principle, I said to myself all night as I tried to find a place in the bed where sleep would bless my churning mind. After a time the words became a rhythm in my head—*Prin-ci-ple, Prin-ci-ple*, like the wheels on the train I could hear on clear nights. I finally dropped into a restless sleep where I saw a crowd of women keeping me from Heber. They pushed me away and held his hands in vise grips. *He's ours now*, they said. *He's mine*, I shouted back, *he's mine!* I shouted all night in my dreams.

I washed the breakfast dishes, my dishcloth circling to the same rhythm I'd heard all night. The sound was so loud I couldn't pay attention to my unkempt children—Jethro, whose nose was running, Jonathan, whose face was specked with breakfast cereal. I wanted to give myself over to God and Brigham Young and Heber, but I couldn't, not in my mind, not with my body. This was *my* family. Heber was *my* husband. We didn't need anyone else. Why did we have to do what Abraham did? He lived a long time ago.

I pulled the carrots out of the bin, scraped the skin, then grated them savagely into a bowl. *I won't do it. No one can make me do it.* Then I caught sight of Gunnar with a pile of boards stacked against his house, the hammer in his hand rising and falling into the head of a nail. He seemed to be building a staircase on the side of his house. But there was no door or window or landing anywhere in sight. His stairs had no destination. Just before sunset, he stopped abruptly, carried his tools away, and left seven stairs going nowhere. "What a fool," I said to my reflection in the window. "Men are fools."

During the month of September, Heber decided on the woman he wanted for the second wife the Lord, through the wisdom of the church officials, commanded him to take. Her name was Naomi; she was eighteen years old and had a tiny waist and the beauty of a woman in bloom. "We've come for your blessing," Hebe said softly as the three of us stood together in the parlor.

"You leave me no choice," I said. The girl blushed and moved closer to my husband.

"I've come to love Heber," she said, looking up at him as if he were a lion in full mane. "I know I'll learn to love you, too," she added and blushed again. Right there in my parlor. The three of us.

I tried to remind myself that God works in mysterious ways, but spent many numb hours at the sink, pulling the parboiled skins from tomatoes and peeling cucumbers. Thank goodness for Gunnar.

As the weather was changing, his projects became even more peculiar. The latest was to shingle one of his chimneys with gold-colored tin. One by one, he tapped nails into each shingle until his whole chimney was covered. Through the steam of my boiling cucumbers, I saw him hoisting a blue Swedish flag on his flagpole. Then he fastened a nosegay of cut paper flowers—pink, blue, yellow—beneath the finial. I almost burned my chin in the rising steam trying to figure what he was up to.

That night, after we lowered the flame on our bedside lamp, I rolled over to face Heber. "Shame, wasting a life like that," I said.

"What life?" Heber said, yawning and folding his reading spectacles on the lamp table.

"Our neighbor's. Have you seen those paper nosegays on his chimney?"

"You are endlessly curious about that man, aren't you? Kiss me goodnight, my Anna." He kissed my forehead. I kissed the top button of his garments. Then I rolled on my back and found the best part of my pillow.

"Those flowers must be for the lost sweetheart, I think. I'd like to be loved like that." All I could hear was Heber's steady, relieved-to-be-close-to-sleep breathing.

"My life is wasted, too," I said, knowing my words were turning to vapor in Heber's ears. "Me being replaced by another woman, especially someone so young and attentive to your every need. She makes me feel like her mother. And you could be her father. That's not right, Heber. The way you look at her. That's the way you used to look at me."

Heber breathed deep from his chest. He was gone, and I was left with the raging feelings that wouldn't give me rest. *I can't do this, God; I can't.* But after I said that so many times, my mind wandered to what Gunnar's sweetheart had been like. If she were a beauty men adored, if she were pock-faced or shy, a burgher's or a poor farmer's daughter? What about Gunnar could have captivated her? And if he loved someone once, why wouldn't he notice anyone else, especially me, out in my yard every day? I felt like the invisible cloth of the emperor's new clothes when Gunnar wouldn't look up and acknowledge me standing there, trying to break the silence with a bunch of radishes in hand, pulled just for him.

As soon as Heber would be finished remodeling the small home on Fourth South Street for his second wife-to-be, about late November he judged, the marriage would take place in the new temple. I'd get to stand in one of the marriage rooms where the two of them would kneel and gaze at each other over the altar, their longing observable in the space between them. I'd be asked to accept this woman as Heber's wife. And because I honored God's wisdom more than my own, I'd give my husband away to another woman, to God's kingdom here on earth. But why?

This was *my* family! My heart was an empty leaden bowl as I stood at my kitchen window and watched autumn leaves float to the ground. And it weighed even more when I tried to keep busy—pulling strings from beans, teaching numbers to the twins, watching what Gunnar did next. This time he was standing on his front porch with a pair of scissors in his hand, shaping hearts and flying birds out of paper, gluing them to his window pane. I was mesmerized by the care he took with the tiny scissors as he trimmed the rounded arcs. He was like an overgrown child, so much larger than the task he was performing.

I wanted to go to him, comfort him, pull him away from the wasteland of his futile projects. But Jethro came down with a fever that same day. I only watched Gunnar from the bedroom window while I cooled my son's head with a wet washcloth. After dragging a ladder to the side of his house, he went back inside and brought out a large framed picture. He climbed to the roof, hammered a long nail into one of the sheets of tin on the chimney, and hung the picture way up high. I couldn't make out what it was until later that afternoon when I went out for Jethro's tonic. Hung at the top of his chimney was a brown sepia tintype of Gunnar's house. Mounted on both sides of the frame were more nosegays of paper flowers—more pink, blue, lemon yellow petals cut from stiff paper and wired together.

When I returned from the chemist's, I decided to be bolder with Gunnar. *Do unto others*, I thought. He must want some company. A friend. Soon, I promised myself.

A more determined autumn moved into the valley that night. The wind picked up after sundown. It blew especially hard after I went to bed, hooting around the corners of the house and keeping me from sleep. I reached over for comfort, but before my hand reached the other side of the bed I remembered Heber was working late at her house-to-be. I listened for the sound of his hammer on the wind. Maybe it would float into the bedroom and haunt me and make me cry again, but instead I heard singing in between the gusts. Swedish words in a sweet high voice. The sound pierced into my loneliness, and I turned the warming brick with my left foot to find the remaining heat.

Turning on my stomach and folding the pillow over my ear, I could still hear the high, penetrating song filtering through the dark. "Close your window, Gunnar," I said out loud. "I don't want to hear your pining!" The chilly night was inappropriate for love songs. I rolled toward Heber's empty spot and circled my non-existent husband with one arm. No response. He could be tender, but he'd never sung love songs to me—five years in the clay country, four children, two miscarriages, always backbreaking work to do. As I nestled against Heber's pillow held close to my breasts, I envisioned a princess in the dark in a dense forest. She had tree-length hair. She was dressed in white, waiting in a tower for a voice to call her name and nothing but her name. *Anna*, I heard on the wind. *Anna*, a part of Gunnar's wistful melody until Heber trudged up the stairs, sat on the bed to unlace his boots, and fell into the mattress and quick sleep.

The snow came that next day.

Through a screen of gentle flakes, I watched Gunnar from my upstairs bathroom window. I brushed my long, dark brown hair while he pulled a rocking chair from inside his house, sat on his front porch, wrapped himself in a wool shawl, and sanded a piece of wood resembling half a flower vase. His knees covered with a ragged quilt, he sat there the entire day as the snow deepened, smoothing the wood patiently. From various windows of my house, sometimes holding Jethro, whose fever was close to breaking, sometimes standing with a finger across my lips, I watched him rub the surface as if it were a baby's skin. Finally, as the blurry sun dropped behind the Oquirrhs, he glued the vase to his front door. Then, through the steel blue light, I saw him stuff a bouquet of paper flowers into the vase, probably pink, blue, and yellow, though the dusk made them colorless.

I knew it was time for me to go to him. I'd rise early the next morning, in enough time to bake bread before the house woke.

I unlatched the gate carefully and balanced on my toes to keep the new snow out of my shoes. The sidewalk seemed long. Kicking against the porch step to shake the snow from my shoes, I noticed something I couldn't have seen from my window. The outline of a heart and the initials GS and AS were carved into the porch pillar; tiny squares of blue paper had been glued together in the shape of a mosaic bird perched at the top of the heart.

After knocking three times, I called his name. "Brother Swenson, it's your neighbor, Sister Crandall." I knocked again; still no answer. "Please answer, Brother Swenson, it's Anna Crandall. I have bread for you."

I was ready to bend down and leave the bread wrapped in the flour sack towel, though I hated to leave it out in the cold just fresh from the oven, when I saw a tiny opening in the door, one eye peering out. I swallowed and nodded my head in greeting. "This is for you, Brother Swenson. I thought I should say hello after all this time being your new neighbor."

The door opened wider. Standing a good foot above my head, Gunnar Swenson stared out at me. His pale blue irises looked like star sapphires. His coarse blonde hair had stubborn cowlicks sticking out in spikes. I felt my chest constricting.

"Anna?" he asked.

"Yes. Anna Crandall."

"Anna?" His white blonde eyebrows faded into his pale face and all I could see were his eyes, the centers laced with spidery white threads. They frightened me.

"I'm Anna Crandall. We moved in last spring. I'm sorry to be so long in saying hello."

"Anna?" he said again. "Why did you leave me? Did you fall off the boat?"

"No," I laughed. "I've never been on a boat. I'm just Anna Crandall. Your neighbor." I pointed to my house.

"Anna. Come in." He trembled like a leaf in the wind. Only frail things were supposed to tremble like that.

Before I allowed myself to cross the threshold, I examined the interior, dark and close smelling. His boots sounded hollow-heeled as he crossed the room and fingered paper flowers stuffed into vases of every kind—quart jars, olive jars, ceramic candy dishes. In some places the wire stems of the paper flowers were stuck into modeling clay to hold them erect.

"Come in."

I held onto the frame of the door for as long as I could before my feet walked into a different world. As I closed the door behind me to keep the cold from Gunnar's already frigid room, I felt an overwhelming iciness.

The ceiling was covered with nosegays of paper flowers, the same pink, blue, and yellow, stiff-papered flowers gathered into bouquets on the chimney and the front door. Each nosegay was fastened upside down to the ceiling to form a canopy. Spun spider threads ornamented the blossoms and gave them a silvery, wispy look. A grayed lace curtain divided the living room from his bed. Two windows, a mantel, a miniature chest of drawers, a small cast iron stove, and one rocking chair, the cane seat of which looked like a bowl for tired bones settled deep between the frame—all seemed incidental in this sea of flowers.

"I have flowers for you," Gunnar said, his eyes not registering my face but looking past my shoulder into another reality. "I have poems. Sit down, Anna."

He pushed the rocking chair close to me and reached over to an alabaster knob on a small drawer and slid it squeaking out of its place. He lifted a yellowed piece of paper, which was folded into a square inch and curled at the corners.

"We've been hoping to see you over at church, Brother Swenson. Everyone wants to get to know you."

"Church?"

"The church, the ward house. You remember."

"Was ten years ago I come from Sweden. Missionaries tell me about Zion, and then I meet you on the boat, Anna. And then you go away."

"Anna Crandall. I'm your neighbor. I just moved here with my husband last spring. Heber and I've been talking how we should get over here and get to know you, but I got caught up with my children, my preserves and garden and settling in. Please forgive me."

All the time I talked, Gunnar was unfolding this tiny square of paper. He used his fingernail to peel each fold from another. Intent on his work, he hadn't heard a word from me. I wanted him to look up so I could say, *Hello from your neighbor*, and be on my way, but he didn't offer me the chance. He picked at the paper carefully. It looked as if it would split instantly with rough handling, especially at the folds. Gunnar finished the delicate operation and started to read without giving me the opportunity to leave his house.

"Anna, many years I say, Anna, fill my days with your smell. The moon changes while I wait, fullness to slivers. I feel the slivers of you in my heart that won't let you be gone from me. Never will you be without flowers."

Gunnar looked up at his ceiling and counted the nosegays hanging there. "Twenty-four, twenty-five," finally "thirty-seven." Then his white-blue eyes turned in my direction, but focused over my shoulder on some place far from this room. Spiked star-eyes filled with visions of flying birds. Gunnar was shaking, this big man who should have been telling everyone what to do. This massive body, which could have its way with people in any dispute, shook as if there were no warm place anywhere.

"Brother Swenson," I said. "Do you see this bread? I baked it for you. I made it with honey."

"I wait for you on the ship. I wait by the rail on the port side. I walk back and forth until Orion goes down to the water. You say you will come and be my bride in Zion. Why you go, Anna? Do you fall in the water? I listen for your voice, 'Gunnar, save me. Gunnar,' but I don't hear you, so maybe you go straight to the bottom."

Maybe I should have eased out the door, but I watched him tremble, like I myself had done in my bed at night. "Gunnar," I said firmly, forgetting propriety. "Listen to me."

"Anna, I keep calling. You don't answer."

I bent forward to pull myself out of the chair, to reach out and take his hand. I didn't think about it or I wouldn't have done it, but I stood right up to him and took his hand, as big as a calf's head, into my small ones. "Gunnar," I stood on my tiptoes. "Listen to me."

He turned to pick up a vase full of flowers. "For you, Anna."

"I am not your Anna. I'm your neighbor."

"My Anna." He covered his ears with his forearms, burying his head between his elbows. "No talk."

When his hands fell back to his sides, I held them again and stroked the tissue paper skin and the blue veins. I held his hand to my cheek and warmed it. "You are so cold, Gunnar. Why don't you light a fire?"

"Now you are here, Anna, I light a fire."

"Why don't you come out to church, Gunnar? There are other women who need love."

"We need a fire, Anna, to keep you warm. I keep you warm. You'll be happy here."

Gunnar bent over the hearth to a stack of split logs mummified in spider webs. Cupping his hands into a small bucket, he transferred dry pine needles into a nest between the logs. Then he pulled open another drawer and unravelled stacks of scrap paper, blue, pink, and yellow, placing them carefully over the logs. He fumbled in a small glass for a match and struck it on one of the fireplace bricks. He stood there, holding the match between his fingers, letting the fire burn until it charred his fingertips.

"Gunnar!" I said. "Drop it on the fire." He smiled at me, the kind of smile where one's face belongs to something else. Blue smoke spiralled. He lit another match.

"Do you need help?" I stepped toward him to take the match. He held it up, out of my reach, and smiled that dispossessed smile again. His smiling canceled my wish to put my hands on his shoulders and make him all right; his smiling made me shrink toward the door. He held the match higher and higher, the flame burning close to his fingers again. "Light the fire, Gunnar. I've got to get back now."

"Days go by, I wait," he sang in English. It was similar to the one I heard him singing the other night. "I wait and I wait, and I rock my arms for my love, for my love." As he lit another match, holding it up and away from me, the flame leapt into the bower of flowers, away from Gunnar's hand. The flame curved into the paper stamens and folded petals and browned them, blackened them, and the entire bower of nosegays came alive for the first time.

"Gunnar," I yelled at him. Gunnar watched the flames leap across his flowers. The heat spread to the lace curtain and browned it to ashes that flaked to the floor and drifted onto his bed, sparking the fibers and the rough floorboards to life as well.

"Run, Gunnar!"

And Gunnar lunged forward, suddenly, lunged toward me and grabbed me in his arms. He hugged me until I couldn't expand my ribs to find a breath. "Gunnar!" I tried to scream. And I looked up at him, and his hair was on fire and he seemed an angel of destruction, an angel of the Lord coming to tell the world to obey or be destroyed in the last days.

"I love you, Anna. I prepare for you like the virgins with lamps. You are my love."

I pulled away from him. "We've got to get out of here." But he seemed to have turned to a pillar of stone. His hair was on fire, his feet rooted to the wooden floor. I grabbed the flour sack towel. The bread tumbled to the floor. Wrap Gunnar's head. Stifle the flames. Smother them. But as I reached for Gunnar's head, he put his hands up to keep me away from him.

"Gunnar!" I shouted. "You're burning!"

His huge arms were the masters of the room, the masters of me with my flour sack towel trying to whip the flames from his head. His huge hands, held up as guards, kept me away while the corona of flame burned brightly around his head. The cracks between the floor boards were narrow rivers of flames. The flowers were curling away from their centers, their carefully cut edges crumbling. Anna's bower—bouquets, valentines, bluebirds, poems hidden in drawers, lace hanging to protect the bridal chamber.

"Let me help you," I begged over the crackling of the fire.

He just smiled, oblivious to the fact he was burning alive. And something happened, something so awe-striking I was humbled in that strange house with the paper flowers and folded poems. Gunnar's hair burned like a torch, but the fire didn't touch his face. His face glowed white, and that rocking chair with the sagging seat, it glowed white too, like the great white throne. Gunnar sizzled with whiteness. I could hear that sound and knew I heard the power of God.

"I love you, Gunnar," I said suddenly, surprising myself. I drew close to him and looked into his eyes, filling with the power I sensed in him. "Anna loves you more than anything in the world. I'm here with you."

I put my arms around his waist and held him as if he were the only man I ever loved. He bent to kiss me, the crown of flame on his head. And I felt the fire pass through my lips and deep into me until I was his Anna, his long-sought love dressed in white like the princess with tree-length hair.

"Forever," I said, then broke away, out of the house and the flames, back to the safety of my home. I grabbed my twins into my arms and rocked them while the fire devoured the seven stairs, the gables, Gunnar's tin-covered chimney. I watched the front porch cave in as the neighbors made their too-late attempt at a fire brigade. I didn't offer my help. I held my babies close until there was nothing left to burn.

Gunnar is with me, nonetheless, as I stand at the kitchen window today, wiping plates dry and looking at the charred ruins of his house. I can see him standing in the fire as if nothing could touch him, smiling with the bliss of a thousand years of peace while the house folded into itself and turned his paper garden to ash.

I can feel him, floating by my side, whispering *Anna* in my ear. And in this weak moment, on the morning of the day I'm supposed to go to the temple with Heber and Naomi, I'm almost overcome by the enormity of his devotion.

But as I lift the dripping flatware from the dish drainer, I can see Gunnar's face in flames, finally crumbling to the black ash of obsession. *My Anna, my Anna*—all he can say. All he can think. I want to believe. I want to hear *Anna* in my ear, buzzing in my head. I want someone to love me that way. Only me. Anna, Queen of All Women. But even as I pray in my secret heart for such purity, I have questions. Wiping a spoon with my checkered dishtowel and dropping it into the wooden drawer, I wonder.

These dishes aren't mine; the house over my head is a loan; the children are God's. Heber is a gift.

"Not my will, but thine," I say to myself as Heber opens the door for us to walk to Naomi's new house and then to the temple. I say it again as I watch Heber and Naomi kneel across the altar from each other, fresh devotion on their faces.

I don't cry. I don't recoil. I take Naomi's hand in mine as she stands. The new wife. The new possibility. I close my eyes and take a deep breath, inhaling God's mysteries.

A Brief History of Seagulls:
A Trilogy with Notes

In the spring of 1848, the Mormon pioneers planted crops after suffering great hunger during the first winter in the Salt Lake Valley. As the crops ripened, hordes of devouring crickets descended upon them from the foothills east of the valley. The saints fought them with clubs, fire and water ... their prayers for deliverance from almost sure starvation were answered when thousands of seagulls came to feed on the crickets.

—Inscription on *Seagull Monument*, Temple Square, Salt Lake City

She watched the first cricket hop onto her curtains—the first and only lace curtains in the Salt Lake Valley, year of our Lord 1848, Lucy Pettingill, proud owner who'd fallen into boasting and self-glorification because of her new possession. As the cricket trespassed across edelweiss blossoms, diamonds and ovals, stems and leaves delicately woven into lace, it showed no respect.

"How dare you?" she said loudly, though the cricket seemed immune to the intensity of her words, its grass-thin legs claiming new territory with every step, its antennae probing wildly.

The curtains had arrived the week before. All the way from Chicago—packed into a strong, brown box, carted to a river boat, stuffed into a saddlebag, warmed by the foaming sides of a horse galloping across the plains to the Territory of Deseret. Lucy unwrapped the package as if she'd never seen a package before, unfolded the curtains as if they might break, and lifted them to the light of the oilskin-covered window. "I've never seen anything so beautiful, Charles." Draping a panel over her hair and around her shoulders, she'd held it tight with a knotted fist—the most precious of shawls. Then she veiled her face.

"I'm Scheherazade, Charles. An Arabian princess surrounded by hanging fuchsia and roses, gazing at shallow pools filled with the fragrance of floating lotus."

She turned dreamily in place—a music box princess—then eased the lace to her shoulders. Charles brushed her lips lightly at the corner of her mouth. She cooed, but then a question popped into her mind.

"How did you make this happen?" The shawl slid to the crook of her elbows.

He palmed her shoulders with his large hands, then wrapped her in his arms. "The sun can tell me the time."

"Your grandfather's watch?" She pushed away to examine his eyes, then thrust her hand into the empty packet where he usually kept his watch.

"I wanted you to be happy."

"But you loved that watch."

"Don't worry." He tucked her under his arm. "Even if the Indians were smart enough not to claim this desolate valley for themselves, we'll make it blossom. And when we do ..." He patted his hip pocket.

"You are love, Charles." She nuzzled his ear.

"As you are." He kissed the hollow of her cheek.

Charles was the kind who saw God's face everywhere—in clouds and in the waving grass of the plains they'd crossed together. But Lucy hadn't been so sure about the presence of God in everything until she hung her lace curtains. While Charles weeded in the communal field, Lucy discovered God through an oval in the lace. He was smiling as if to say, "You are blessed among women. No one else has the bounty you've been given." His eyes filtered through the curtains, patterned the hard earth floor, and filled her with his presence—the Divine, the

Beautiful, the Great, and the Good. Lucy shared this story with neighbors, discreetly, of course.

But now, in her one room shaped from the hard earth, she could only see a leggy insect with probing antennae, treading on the precious threads, cocking its head from side to side, considering her curtains. An insidious little creature with ugly, hostile eyes.

She'd heard rumors of crickets all morning long, but hadn't seen any until about an hour ago when she carried water to the raspberry starts—her work assignment on Tuesdays and Fridays. They were landing on everything green—stalks of corn, curlicues of bean plants, swollen buds with squash blossoms inside. At first they landed politely, genteel summer visitors. Then, all too quickly, a wall of crickets approached from the east, thick and dark. The day turned into cricket night. The vibration of the insects' wings and jaws and legs and the human shouts of "Crickets!" grew louder each minute. "The crickets will have everything!" people shouted.

With her water bucket in hand, Lucy watched Brother Kenton hop from foot to foot as crawling things swarmed. She heard Sister Whitesides shouting for kindling for a fire wall. She saw the Esplin sisters unrolling a bolt of muslin and stretching it taut to scoop crickets up and away from the ground.

Lucy pulled the tea towel tucked in her skirt waist, the only weapon she had. She dropped her bucket and ran to join the frenzy, scattering bunch after thick bunch of crickets with the snap of her towel. Lucy, Charles, and their neighbors stomped their feet, jumped on crickets, squashed them with their shoes, their hoes, their shovels, their blankets, their brooms—anything they could find. But the crickets only multiplied.

Lucy kept forgetting her work in the field to look back at her home. She felt a knot in her stomach—a warning. "I'll be back," she shouted to Charles. Before he could tell her it was no use, she was running to the end of the row and stumbling across rock-hard caliche and stones and brittle sage, crossing the bleak stretch between her and her adobe house.

"My curtains!" she worried as she ran.

As soon as she crossed the threshold, she grabbed her broom and swept crickets out the door, but each stroke pulled more of them inside than out. And now she was face to face with an impudent cricket testing the worth of her curtains with ridiculous legs.

"How dare you," she shouted again, flipping at the insect with her trusty towel. The cricket only hesitated in the air before fluttering back again. Then there were two, and three, and then a hundred trespassing on the field of lace. Lucy brushed them away with the flat of her hand, but the crickets swarmed over her forearm, shoulders, her hair, and she was covered with a living blanket of seething crickets.

"You!" she screamed. "Stop!" She slapped at her arms and her face and her neck. Frantically, she shook the curtains with both hands to stop the thousands of jaws from snipping and chewing. As she did, the network of fine thread gave way, not unlike burning wood disintegrating into ash. The exquisite circles and diamonds enlarged to monstrous holes. Her field of *fleur-de-lys*, edelweiss, and lily of the valley was a field of air.

Just as quickly, the crickets were gone, leaving her with the same life as before: a shabby one-room adobe house with hard clay floors and the boiling desert outside. The buffer between her and the harsh landscape had been destroyed. Her curtains everyone admired, even coveted, though no one was supposed to covet in this community which prized obedience to God's laws above all else, were nothing but skeletal threads. Was there such a thing as a good life when so much destruction was possible? But her thoughts were interrupted by a new sound she'd never heard before. Something beating the sky.

Looking out the window, she saw the sun darkening again in midday. Lucy bolted outside to watch thousands of seagulls flapping their wings, spreading them wide for landing, aiming their slanted feet to overturned soil. There were more birds than she'd ever seen, folding their wings to their sides, striking madly at the ground with their beaks. When she looked up again, she saw something larger in the backdrop of the cluttered sky, something that appeared to be angels with white- and silver-tipped wings. The judgment of God filled the sky. Destroying angels opened the folds of their robes and dropped seagull after seagull to the earth. While her neighbors shouted, "The birds are eating the crickets. Can you believe the birds are eating the crickets?" Lucy was speechless.

Legs and heads of crickets dangled from the birds' beaks. Black juice stained their yellow bills. One of them looked in Lucy's direction, as if considering her. Then it turned to peck at another cricket.

Everyone seemed stunned, watching the gluttonous feast which continued for the rest of the day until the sun finally slipped behind the mountains. The seagulls followed. Sated. The fields were silent.

"Our crops," Charles shouted, his face covered with strings of sweat and dirt and a wide grin as he ran across the desert in the changing light, a triumphant warrior. He circled her hips with his arms and lifted her from the ground. "We can eat. We'll survive." He turned a few more times before noticing Lucy's mood.

She held her arms stiff against his, not smiling in return. "The curtains," she said with an empty voice.

"The curtains?"

"Yes."

He set her on the ground. He pulled off his hat. "The curtains," he said again, sinking to his haunches, elbows on his knees, one hand kneading the brim of his hat. Charles looked into his wife's lavender eyes. He wiped his forehead with the back of his hand while she gathered her apron into both of hers.

"Curtains don't matter as much as food, I guess" he said, uneasily considerate of her feelings even though his chest pounded with the power of the things he'd seen.

"Those curtains were everything to me." She looked white and pale and small in the emptiness of the backlit desert, unaware that the sky behind her was filling with brilliant light. "I thought God loved me."

"I'm sorry, Lucy." Charles stood up and reached into his pocket where his watch should have been. His hand lingered in the empty space, thumb and forefinger rubbing together, but this was no time for regret. He pulled his hand from his pocket and threw his hat in the air. "We've just seen a miracle. Whoo-ee."

Tears blurred her eyes as Lucy bent her head back to follow the flight of the hat into the brilliant orange sky. But then she blinked to clear her vision. The swirling clouds seemed to be swallowing the speck of a hat. The sky had become a mosaic of *fleur de lys*, edelweiss, ovals, diamonds. Her eyes widening in amazement, she witnessed the veil between heaven and earth, the thin membrane protecting the power and the glory, the face of the Almighty. And God was smiling through the openwork of the clouds. "Consider this bounty," she thought she heard him say.

As Charles's hat fell back to the field and he ran to retrieve it from the tangles of a ravaged squash plant, she hugged her arms to her chest and cradled herself. She bit her lip and searched for words to say to God and to Charles, who was tossing his hat up yet another time like a boy in a bubble of ecstasy.

II

In 1848, seagulls vomited grasshoppers into the Great Salt Lake, then returned for more.

—Fife Folklore Collection, Utah State University

Anabrus simplex, better known as Mormon Crickets (though they are actually grasshoppers), have been known to migrate in bands a mile wide and ten miles long when spring conditions are mild and dry for several years. They don't travel during overcast or wet weather. Otherwise, they travel 1/2 to 1 mile a day in the summer.

—Salt Lake Tribune, 1989

Max cleared his throat. He tapped his toe. He'd been waiting for too long at the checkout counter of the Big Bear Feed & Grain Supply. Sheila, the clerk and his estranged wife, was talking on the telephone. She was also leaning over the counter and exposing the tops of her ice cream cone breasts as if to remind Max what he was missing. She did look slimmer than usual in her hot pink dress, a velvet ribbon choker around her neck. She must have bought the outfit for her new life. Bleached the gray in her hair, too.

"Those'll be in on Monday," she said as she stood up, arched her back, and hung the phone on its cradle. She poked a yellow purchase order onto a spindle, adjusted the volume on the stereo to a higher level, and then, after looking slowly to the right, as if there might be something more important happening elsewhere, she yawned and folded her arms. "So, you've got cricket problems, Max?" She patted one of the bags of steam-rolled wheat loaded with carbaryl that sat on the counter.

"No, Sheila. This poison is for my health." Max tucked in the back of his shirt with two hands, sniffed, and lifted his chin like he had a cramp in his neck.

"I've been selling tons of this stuff for the past few days. Must be potent." She smiled her Sheila smile, a little bit crooked, though Max noticed the vertical lines above her lip were getting deeper. "But wouldn't it be better to leave the crickets to the seagulls?"

"Seagulls. What a joke!"

"You never did believe in miracles, did you, Max?" She checked to see if customers were on their way to the checkstand. A few people milled at the display where high beam flashlights were being offered at a limited low price, but no one seemed to be hurrying in the direction of the checkout counter. "We always did argue about God and what he could do."

"You and your miracles, Sheila."

"Not now, Max. Nobody needs your lip right now."

Max put his thumbs behind his belt and felt good about the way he was giving it to Sheila, getting a rise out of her still after twenty-two years of marriage. She needed to know he was just as much a live wire as ever. Still virile. Still strong. He licked the tips of his moustache and changed the position of his feet. Two solid boots on the ground. He folded his arms. One big mass of man.

Sheila hummed as she put her hands on her hips and shook her shoulders ever so slightly to the mariachi music on the radio. The Spanish hour on KPGU-FM was programmed once a week for the migrant workers who'd decided to become citizens and grow something that belonged to them for a change. Sheila listened to catch on to the language, like her Spanish-I teacher suggested. She also convinced her boss that one hour a week was good for business. "Mutual respect," she told him. He named her clerk of the month after that.

"Since you're buying carbaryl, Max, you'll probably want to hear what I heard yesterday."

"You know me, sweetheart. Always ready and waiting."

"You're such a lover boy, Max." She swayed ever so slightly behind the counter, cha cha cha, one, two, lifting her freckled, leathery arms like horizontal wings. The years of sun and wind had imprinted themselves in her skin, even in the paleness of her eyes. She'd worked hard on the farm.

"That I am, Ms. Sheila." Max leaned his hands flat into the counter, rested his wallet on the scratched formica, tried to gauge the appropriate distance from this woman who was supposed to be his wife.

She was holding out longer than he ever thought she could. When she said she was leaving him, he was sure she'd be back after a week's time, at the most. But she'd been living at her sister's for five months now, not even calling him to help with her car, that old junker. She always said she liked how he did odd jobs. How handy he was. "So what's this you were going to tell me?"

"Did you know that ... " She leaned across the counter to whisper, cupping one hand around her mouth in that flirty way of hers. "Crickets are cannibals. They eat their diseased and crippled and dead. Bait 'em and they go especially berserk." She tapped her pencil on the counter to the south-of-the-border beat still playing on the radio.

"I'm delighted to hear the news." Max tipped back the brim of his straw hat, revealing his albino white forehead. He scratched that soft stretch of pure white skin and noticed that Sheila's pretty lips were separated as she watched him put his hat back in place. He wanted to stare at those full, heart-shaped lips, pucker lines and all. "I'll do anything to get rid of those creepy things. They've stripped the alfalfa, even the sagebrush and the willows in the south pasture. Before it's too late, I've got to save my wheat."

"Rambo Max," Sheila said, scanning the bar code on the bulky bags of steam-rolled wheat. "The only way you know how to do life. If only you could have believed in a few miracles. In something besides your own efficiency."

"I'll ignore that comment, being's I've heard it before. You used to like my style." Sheila's eyes were flat and foreign when he scanned her face for clues. No response. "But you might be interested to know your beloved seagulls flew over my land this morning."

"*Our* land, my Max," Sheila said as she slid the 50-lb. bags of wheat off the counter and back into Max's cart. "It's still our land. In addition to Spanish, I'm taking an assertiveness training class at the high school."

"I stand corrected, darlin'."

"Don't *darlin'* me." Sheila's eyes were narrowing in a way that caused a familiar discomfort to rise inside Max. They reminded him of that last breakfast of burned pancakes and over-fried eggs on a large blue plate. She'd slid them in front of him like he was the enemy. "*Eat this, you turd.*"

Sheila's words had caught him by surprise, coarse as they were coming out of her mouth, but that was her final say on the final day of matrimonial bliss—the end of the time when he could do no wrong, when Sheila looked up to him, and when she said she was sorry for whatever happened, no matter whose fault. He'd thought a lot about this Big Change in Sheila. Contrary to public and Sheila's private opinion, he'd been doing some thinking on the subject—the whys and the wherefores of this change in his wife.

"Where are the seagulls when we need them?" Charlie Santos, a squat farmer with a pencil moustache, arrived at the checkout stand with three bags of the same treated wheat in his cart, a paint roller and two brushes in his hand. "I just came over from I-15. You oughta see the greasy mess over there. Crickets mashed like potatoes. Department of Agriculture measured 235 per square yard."

"I don't want to hear the word seagulls," Max mumbled. "Don't anybody talk about seagulls."

"So what's the matter with you?" Sheila said. "You know how the seagulls saved the pioneers."

"Charlie, my man," Max said, shifting until one hip held his weight against the counter. "You be the ref. Do you really believe the seagulls saved the pioneers?"

"Doesn't everybody?" Charlie laid his supplies on the counter and took a toothpick from his shirt pocket. "There's a monument on Temple Square up in Salt Lake, for heck sakes."

"Charlie, those famous seagulls flew into town this morning. Did they show up at your place?"

"What can I say, Max? You know I ain't too religious."

"Should that matter?" Max had an I-know-something-you-don't-know look in his eyes. His face was alive with anticipation, his eyebrows poised for action.

"There were thousands of them, I tell you, flapping their wings and filling the sky." Max had a way of getting bigger, of using the whole length of his arms and hands, when he told a story. He spread his arms open.

"I got a lump in my throat when I saw 'em, Charlie." He pointed to his throat. "There were so many. So much bird racket. 'I'm in the middle of a miracle,' I said to myself. Crickets've been eating every green thing in my south pasture and here the mighty seagulls show up to save the rest of my crops. 'Wouldn't Sheila be out of her mind about this?' I thought."

Max stood his full six-foot-three with a look of astonishment on his face, his hands raised as if part of the question. "But guess what?"

"Tell us, Big Boy," Sheila said. "You've got a sinker in your pocket. I can tell."

"Don't call me *Big Boy* like that, Sheila." He faced off square with her and shook his pointed finger with each syllable he spoke: "Have some re-spect."

"Don't shake your finger at me." Sheila pointed a finger back at him, something she'd never done when she lived at home.

Max remembered how she'd asked him umpteen times not to do that, not to shake his finger at her like she was a child who needed a scolding. Max looked at his finger and then looked over at sheepish Charlie who'd happened into this domestic fireworks show.

"Love," Max said, shrugging his shoulders and grinning at Charlie.

"Love, my foot," Sheila said, twisting the gold-plated heart pin fastened to the front of her velvet choker.

"You're being rude, Sheila. That's not like you."

"And you're not, Max?"

"So you two," Charlie said, patting Max on the shoulder carefully. "I was sort of hoping the seagulls would drop by, even if I don't get out to church all that much. You think this carbaryl'll do the job if they don't, Max?"

"Hell, yes," Max said, growing bigger with every word he spoke. "Hell, yes and hell, yes."

"Excuse me, Max," Sheila said softly, suddenly remembering her commitment to professionalism and customer relations. She was, after all, a service-award-winning clerk after only five months at Big Bear Grain & Feed in Payson, Utah, and she did have two customers at her checkstand. She lowered her head and tilted it to the side. "That *was* rude of me. Max, I know how you hate to be called Big Boy."

Max wanted to get a lock on Sheila's eyes right then. Had he heard right? Did he detect a trace of that rare thing called an apology?

"I better collect from you, Max," Sheila said, no overtones in her voice. "I need to check out Charlie, here. You don't want to be in line all day, do you now, Charlie?" She pulled out one of her charmer smiles.

"Can't say as I do, Sheila." Charlie smiled back, hook, line, and sinker. "But don't let me interrupt anything between you and Max now."

"I need to tell you the rest of the story, Charlie," Max said. "You need to hear this, too, Sheila. You and your devotion to unexplainable things need to hear this." He dropped his hands to his sides. "You don't mind, Charlie. It'll just take a minute."

Charlie picked between two of his molars with his toothpick.

"These birds landed in my field, just like the story goes." Max was back into bigness. "My heart was beating like crazy, being excited to be in a miracle. But get this. This is the pitiful part. They flew in. A big show. But then, after my heart is pounding and I'm thinking every cricket is going to disappear, those suckers only ate a few crickets. I swear. On the Book of Mormon, Bible, and Doctrine and Covenants. They ate crickets for about two minutes at the most, and then they flew over to the sandbars on the river to take a nap. And to think I was ready to believe ..."

Sheila raised one eyebrow and looked square at Max. "They took a nap?"

"Those seagulls tucked their heads under their wings and went to sleep. I swear."

Sheila held on to the edge of the counter with both hands, waiting for words to come. "Maybe ... maybe they flew in from a long distance," she protested. "Maybe they needed to rest before they gorged on crickets. Maybe they'd been eating them all morning and needed a break."

"Keep trying, Sheila."

"Maybe it's the garbage," Sheila said, turning down the volume on the stereo. The news was on. Spanish hour was over. "They hang out at the dumps, you know. That's what's changing everything. The burgers, Cokes, and fries. The preservatives. It's changed all of us. Our minds and our bodies."

Max felt like this was a phoney Sheila talking. Someone with a little bit of night school knowledge acting like she knew something the rest of the world didn't. She'd always loved burgers, Cokes, and fries and had a midsection that was thicker than was good for her because of it. Then she left home and started taking those classes at the high school. But Max refrained from saying anything. He didn't make a smart remark like he would have as few as six weeks ago. He had a head on his shoulders, when all was said and done, and he wanted to make things right again. He chose his words with care.

"So that's the answer, is it?"

"There's nothing wrong with the seagulls, Max," Sheila snapped, taking offense automatically, it seemed to Max. She couldn't stop being angry long enough to recognize his sensitive choice of words and the new tone of his voice. "Stop trying to discredit the seagulls, and me. Leave it alone. You're not going to get me to change my mind. End item. Pay up and let me take care of Charlie. Please."

Despite his good intentions, he felt his temper coming on. His finger was twitching as if it wanted to shake itself at Sheila, scold her, and tell her to come back home and be Sheila—the woman he loved despite everything. Right now. He felt his hands wanting to hook his finger inside the velvet choker that made her look like she was trying to be sixteen and pull her out the door and across the parking lot and kidnap her in his Chevy Dualie. Wrap her in burlap. Keep her quiet for a few days until things returned to normal.

"Rush me right along, Ms. Sheila. Unwilling to hear anything except the sound of your own voice."

"Why is it always the fat lip, Max?" Sheila said, the hot pink of her dress seeming to fade.

Max felt tired. He glanced down at his belly that must have grown while he was standing here. It was sagging. It was tired, too. Too many meals. Too much gravity. How could he have a belly after all the hay bales he tossed into the back of his truck? How could both he and Sheila be getting old? How could they be at such a stupid standoff? He swallowed. He cleared his throat.

"In spite of what you call my fat lip, I'm proud of you, Sheila," he said with no trace of his usual sarcasm. "Taking classes and all."

Sheila's eyes didn't pop out of her head like in the comics, but almost. "Did I hear what you just said?"

"Everybody needs to stand up for themselves. I've been thinking about it, believe it or not." Max pulled the bills out of his wallet—a thick stack of twenties. "What do I owe you?"

Sheila's whole body softened like ice cream left out of the refrigerator. "What do you owe me?" She said the words slowly, wistfully, as they stood across from each other. She wasn't laughing. Her tone had changed to the softest edge Max had heard in a long time—it wasn't even an edge anymore. Their eyes didn't get to point zero right away, but then, they met.

Sheila's deep brown eyes made Max consider miracles—the way she was looking at him now, the first he'd seen anything like that for a good long time. It reminded him of the way she'd looked at him when she thought he was the best, even the greatest. He wanted to feel the soft press of her body, himself melting inside her. That was a miracle, if he could call anything a miracle.

"When are you comin' home, Sheila?" he almost said, the thought crowding his brain. Instead he looked at the red numbers on the electronic cash register and put two twenties on the counter instead of into Sheila's hand. Maybe next time. Next time for sure.

"Let me get your change," Sheila said, her eyes lowered to protect what was happening in them.

"I'd be obliged," Max lifted his hat from his forehead to air the sweatband.

"Good luck with the crickets, Max. I mean it."

"Thanks." He slowly rolled the cart toward the door, wishing he weren't walking out the door, wishing he had a reason to buy something else. "Hey, Charlie," he called back to the counter. "Get those bugs."

"Will do, Max. You, too."

"Don't lose faith in the seagulls, Max," Sheila called after him. "Miracles do happen."

He lifted the back wheels of his shopping cart over the store's aluminum weatherstripping and clattered across the parking lot to his Chevy, all the time groping for his keys, all the time wondering.

III

To: Gerald Blake, Davis County Environmental Health
         Department
From: Colonel Geoffrey Stevenson, Hill Air Force Base

We've got to solve the seagull problem NOW. Another F-16 was damaged last Monday on the runway, due to the seagulls at the Davis County Landfill. We can't keep endangering our jets to the tune of $30 million a piece.

Hank Steeves, lieutenant colonel, flipped the thumb switch on his throttle to slow his F-16. Below him, the Great Salt Lake sprawled in the late summer afternoon while the sun's reflection on the water flashed Morse code. *Dot dot dot, dash dash dash, dot dot dot.*

He cupped a hand over the receiver and shouted over the chatter inside his helmet: "I'm back, Utah." But no one said, "Welcome home, Steeves." Only the chatter in his headset—"Check in at 5. Helicopter hovering around flight line. Can give you clearance for runway 29"—the never-ending buzz near civilian territory. Because he was checking the com dials, he didn't see the signal from the sun on the water.

He wished there weren't so many voices vying for his attention. So many planes needing directions to traverse the sky. So many air traffic controllers. Sometimes the noise was too much for him. There was no space for any thought at all up in the big blue.

"Bingo fuel," the seductive recording of a computerized female spoke to him. "Bingo fuel." But he knew he had enough to make it back to Hill. He'd been farther out before when he'd heard the automatic warning.

"Crosswind on Runway 15." Steeves knew how to sort out the information meant for him. Runway 15 belonged to Salt Lake International, not the base. "Hold in present pattern."

Here he was, sitting at the tip of a long $30 million pencil, high out in the open, but still enclosed in a bubble. Even with the fancy high tech surrounding him, more information about G-forces than he could ever use, he was still a small human being with two legs and two arms, a torso, and a head. And even though these machines were smarter than any man could ever be, none of this equipment could come close to being a bird. Wasn't it more impressive, when all was said and done, to fly quietly on two wings and a breast full of feathers, every feather designed for the express purpose of flight, no hard metal, no deafening roar of engines?

He looked to the side to see if just maybe the wings of his F-16 were flapping, performing some new exotic high-tech feat he hadn't known about. Then, laughing at himself, he tilted his head back to see the wide expansive sky, so huge up here.

"Salt Lake International. Check in at 7 ..." The jumble of frequencies crowded back into his awareness as he flew over the mosaic of the Oquirrhs, the Uintahs, the snow, desert, water, Antelope Island, sage, and salt-stung sand. Flatness. Spareness. Aloofness. A land needing no one, wanting no one, asking nothing.

"Transfer to Hill controller." He recognized his orders from Salt Lake International, handing him over to the base. He banked slightly, and, for just a brief second, the chaos in his headset stopped and everything seemed quieter than the inside of a crystal. Steeves was out of time, above a voiceless world. He was floating. He felt the wind whispering his name. *"Come to me."*

Then he saw the seagulls. The seagulls he'd heard about as a boy. Every July 24th, Pioneer Day, some Sunday school teacher pulled out the story of the seagulls who saved the pioneers. He never had figured out why there were seagulls in this desert, so far inland, but here they were. Seagulls in airspace, disinterested in what a traffic controller might have to say.

They were white and whiter, the whitest, maybe because of the reflection of the sun on the lake. And they had wings of their own, unlike Steeves, unlike the jet that had mock, stiff wings copied from birds.

Steeves could see two gulls catching a current, dipping, rising, falling with the wind. If only he had a button he could push, one that would cut the engines and let the plane catch a current, let him float over the lake in silence with the birds. But all of a sudden they were flying too close to his plane, pulled in like magnets.

He heard a sickening noise, something that wasn't coming out of his headset. It wasn't the sound of gulls crying into the wind, making sea sounds over this dead inland sea. It was the sound of what was happening to the birds. Red lights flashed. He heard the coughing and smothering and whining of his engines. He felt the nose of his plane dip awkwardly toward the Great Salt Lake, toward the water, toward the bottom of the lake where it would be buried in brine.

Please no. Not this. Oh shit, no. No.

Engines. Re-start. He pushed the emergency starter. Nothing happened. No response from the engines. "Bird strike! Bird strike!" he barked into his headset.

Plane going down. Punch out. I can't punch out. My plane. Oh God in Heaven, why me?

Punch out, Steeves. Now.

I can't leave this baby. No pilot worth his salt leaves Uncle Sam's money at the bottom of a lake. Me, standing in front of the squadron wearing cement shoes. They'll bury me with the plane. A bird, I'll say. A little bird and so much science. Not me. No.

But I've got water below. No civilians to worry about. Time to do it. I can't.

There's no choice.

Visor down. Head back or I smash my backbone. Oh, Mother Mary and Jesus, here I come.

What if I don't make it? What if I buy the farm from The Old Man in the Sky?

Elbows in. Tight to the sides.

He's pulling on the ejection handle between his knees, the yellow rubber loop designed to keep his elbows by his sides. The seat blows. The spike at the top of the chair splits the bubble wide open, and he's blasting through dense matter into no matter at all. The shattered remains of the canopy blast into the air and catch sunlight and whirl like scattershot in a cyclone and surge up before they float down. He's sailing out of the top of the F-16 as it drops its nose farther and draws a long line beneath him, leaving him. The gyro rocket in the seat is turning him upright, the drogue chute slowing him down. As his own parachute opens and the seat drops away, he's flying. He holds out his arms and flaps them in the quiet of high sky. His arms have no feathers to spread. His legs are a useless tail. But he knows what it is to be part of the wind, to feel the fierce chill on his face, to drop with grace from the sky. For a brief moment, his wish is granted, and he knows the province of birds.

TV NEWS REPORT:

The seagulls are gone from the Davis County Landfill after a month-long battle. The protected birds that saved the Mormon pioneers in 1848 were driven from the area this morning when marksmen gunned down six of their flock. County officials said they acted on the advice of the Air Force's Bird Air Strike Hazard team—known as BASH—which suggested the birds would leave the area if they saw others in their flock fall. After last week's F-16 crash, caused by a seagull, efforts have been stepped up to remove the birds. Officials have tried firecrackers, recordings of birds in distress, and Zond guns firing at timed intervals to frighten the birds. As many as 25,000 gulls have made the landfill their home, jeopardizing training missions at nearby Hill Air Force Base. By sunset today, only a few stragglers remained.

Prophet by the Sea

One late afternoon as the sun was falling, the prophet with white hair like the mane of a lion walked by the sea with his friend, Fernando. They talked of many things as the water rushed to the soles of their shoes and rushed away again.

"My wife," said Fernando to the prophet, his head and shoulders curving in discouragement. "*Mi Elena*. She will not repent. *Mi Elena hermosa*." He shook his head in sorrow as the wind played with his bead black hair.

"What has she done?" the prophet asked, stopping to watch a sand crab scuttle after the water.

"She insists, my dear *Profeta*, that she speaks not only with God, but God's wife. God is not divided. God is everything together. And besides," Fernando's words tumbled faster, "that is your job to do the speaking. You are God's mouth on earth."

"Do you love each other?" the prophet asked as he watched a sea-gull swoop over their heads, its webbed feet posed for landing, its wings swept back by the wind.

"Of course, dear *Profeta*. We live to give each other comfort, but her ideas fly like birds from a flock." He closed his eyes and drummed his chest with his fingertips.

The prophet put his arm around Fernando's shoulders. "Wanting to know God is a big task, and how can anyone know God who is always unfolding, even me?"

Fernando turned his cheek against the stiff breeze. "I listen to her. But tears find my eyes when I hear her wild parrot words. I want us to be together for eternity."

At that moment, Fernando's long, sad, and beautifully sculpted face reflected the bright orange that tinctured the bottoms of the massive gray clouds. His eyes searched, as if to see the finger of God writing an answer across the sky fast filling with varied ripenesses of peach and gray.

The prophet bent to scoop sand into both hands and let it trickle like fine salt to the beach. Then he rested on his heels, his white hair seeming like a shaded lamp at dusk, the way it glowed as the greater light diminished. Finally, he sat down, untied his shoelaces, removed his socks, and folded them into his simple brown shoes. He rolled up his pant legs, loosened his tie, and wriggled his toes in the cool gray sand.

Fernando returned from his consideration of clouds. "Please tell me what to do."

"Sit by my side." The prophet patted the beach with his hands. "Let's build a castle together. I haven't done that for years."

"Me neither." Fernando stood stiffly in his suit and tie and Sunday best cologne. "But sand castles, my dear *Profeta?*"

"Why not, Fernando?" he said, scooping more sand into both hands and tossing it in the air. "Think how very old this sand must be and of the shoes and feet that have crushed it so fine."

"I can't think of anything except there is so much to do." Fernando paced back and forth on the beach, asserting his finger in the air with each thought. "So many people who need to hear the gospel, my wife to keep in the fold."

"Come build a castle with me. We can dig a moat and maybe add a tower before sunset."

"There is so little time, *mi Profeta.* " And Fernando drove his fingers through his bounteous hair and bowed his head against the palms of his hands. "The sword of justice. It hangs over us."

"I feel your anguish, my brother." His eyes lifted to Fernando's and spoke much more with their silence.

Fernando stopped pacing and thrust his hands into his pockets. He squinted at the sun's furnace burning up the last of the daylight and burnishing his black hair with red streaks. "Don't distract me with those eyes, *mi Profeta*. If a man repenteth not," he held up one fist, "he shrinks from the presence of the Lord and his pain and anguish is like an unquenchable fire, not unlike that fiery ball of sun balancing on the horizon this very moment."

"Fernando, you are a fierce lion." The prophet patted the sand again. "But for one moment, sit by my side."

Fernando smiled, uncovering his straight, narrow teeth. "*Leon de Dio*." He lifted his chin to the West, and his chiseled face, strong cheekbones, and bristled eyebrows were indeed leonine against the blunt slant of light.

"Look!" The prophet burst to his feet, brushing sand from the seat of his pants and keening his head toward the water. Something dark and slow and triangular was rising from the surf. Something amorphous, a creature of the twilight silhouetted in the shade between dark and light.

Fernando and the prophet watched speechlessly as the creature pulled itself slowly onto the beach, water rolling off its sides, water swirling at its feet, part dragon, dragging its belly, lumbering from side to side until it collapsed—its head in the damp sand, its back and sides caressed by fingers of tide.

"*Por Dios!*" yelled Fernando over the sound of the wind and the waves as he struggled to run across the beach in his black patent lace-up shoes that quickly filled with sand. As he ran, the ball of sun suddenly dropped into the ocean, leaving a fan of gold light flecked with fish scale clouds. And as Fernando finally reached the creature on the beach, the wrist of God snapped the fan closed, and it, too, dropped into the void and pulled the day behind it.

The prophet walked calmly behind Fernando, not as young and quick as his friend. As he pulled each footstep from the sucking sand, the night began to claim the sky. In this half light, the prophet's white hair glowed even brighter—a flame on a candle in a large window. A thin, luminous mist surrounded his body. Dark sticks of driftwood reached from the sand like arms asking to be held, but the prophet walked steadily toward the fallen creature.

"*Es leon del mar*," Fernando shouted over the sound of the waves pulling pebbles back to sea. "*Leon marino.*"

"A sea lion, Fernando?"

"*Si. El toro grande.*"

"He's bigger than both of us together, Fernando."

The massive animal's breathing was labored. It rested its head and wrinkled neck in a shallow bowl of beach and glared at the prophet as he knelt by its side. But the bull was too weak to frighten any man or even another sea lion from its territory. Its silky black eyes seemed more liquid than substance.

Fernando tried to kick the sand from the cuffs of his trousers, then bent forward to look as closely as possible. His yellow-knit tie dangled above the sea lion's head like a twisted rag. "He's hurt badly. His neck is torn."

The prophet stroked the exposed side of the bull's head, running his finger down the length of the blunt nose and over the arch of its eye and down to its small flap of an ear. The sea lion tried to bark, but the sound was a weak gesture.

"This is the way of nature," said Fernando, squatting to look into the prophet's face. "He was probably fighting for his territory."

"All the kingdom for territory, then?" the prophet said as he felt the slowly heaving sides of the sea lion beneath his hands. "How human."

"I can't stand to see *el muerte* anytime." Fernando turned his head to watch a wave disperse its foam on the beach. "Even if it is a part of life."

"Death is only a moment, Fernando. You mustn't be afraid."

"But I am afraid, *El Profeta.* This sea lion reminds me the end is close. There's so little time to accomplish what God has asked of me."

"Death is only a door, Fernando. And time is bigger than a clock. There's enough of it to do what you need to do, to accomplish what you're here to accomplish. Trust, my friend."

The prophet rubbed the loose wrinkles on the bull's neck that looked like hills and tight valleys. Lightly, he tracked his finger across the broad gash at the side of its neck and down the length of one whisker. Then he put both hands on the bull's head, closed his eyes, and lifted his face to the sky. His white hair blew like wings and danced with the brisk breeze. He inhaled the ancient smell of the sea. His breath moved with the tide.

"In the name of the holy priesthood, bless my brother, dear God. Bless this creature, its eyes, its heart. Give it strength, in the name of Jesus Christ."

"Jesús. Por favor." Fernando placed his hands in prayer at the center of his chest.

Pushed and pulled by the magnets of heaven, the water came to and went from the shore. The men were still like a painting, their heads bowed over the animal, the prophet's hands gentle on its head. Underneath the upside down bowl of sky where the first star was appearing, his fingers trembled like arrows from the quiver of God. The waves repeated themselves, as if they were the earth's breath. Exhalation, inhalation, the great constancy. This passed through the prophet and through his hands to the great sea lion.

Gradually, the breath of the waves became the breath of the animal. In and out. The huge bull turned its head, rolled back to its stomach, and struggled to lift onto its front flippers. It lifted its body out of the sand, until its neck was once again a massive triangle beneath its whiskers, its nose pointed to the heavens, and its head proud and strong. The sea lion barked crisply before turning to the water's edge and the black stones washed smooth and round like beetles' backs. It pulled itself over the slippery rocks and wet oozing sand to the water.

"Now," said the prophet, sitting back down in the sand as the dark shape of the sea lion sank into the ocean. "Before it's completely dark, will you build a castle with me, Fernando?"

Fernando balanced on one leg and bent to untie his shoe. When the first black patent shoe dropped into the sand in the twilight, it seemed a small boat cutting across an endless sea.

Mormon Levis

Tight, like two long cigarettes rolled in denim. We call them white Levis, Mormon Levis, but they're actually albino beige. I suck in my stomach, zip up my pants on the way to the window in my bedroom, split the venetian blinds to check the night and see if Shelley's pulling into my driveway. Not yet. I walk down the stairs and see my long legs reflected in the mirror at the bottom. Daddy Long Legs. Leggy legs. Legs made for walking and dancing the whole night through.

Where did you say you were going, Mattie? my mother asks as she pretends to dust the piano with the dishtowel in her hands.

To the movie.

What's playing?

A western.

I hear Shelley's horn. Thank heavens. I'm out of here. Out the door. Bye, Mom.

Remember your curfew, Mattie. And don't be chasing after those boys you think are so cool. You know better.

My eyes brush past my mother's eyes and the picture of Jesus on the wall behind her. Sunrays coming out of his head. Light like the sun on his forehead. Jesus is always looking over someone's shoulder it seems. Sure, Mom. Bye.

The door sounds final as I slam it, sealing me off from my house. I'm released into Friday night.

Hey, Wondah Woman, Shelley says after I slam the door of her brown Plymouth that looks like a tank. She backs into the street that separates me from the desert: the rim of Las Vegas, the edge of the plate. My house is in the last subdivision in town. The desert is my front yard.

Hey, Wondah Woman yourself, I say. Tonight's the night.

Shelley turns the radio up until the sound is bigger than the car and the street. *Stairway to Heaven*. I settle back against the seat and drape my arm over the open window. We're off to hunt for Rod and The King, our non-Mormon, forbidden boyfriends. Forget the movie. Find somebody who knows the plot. We're off to the Bright Spot to wait for the boys.

They're at the Tracks right now, the place where the manly men of Las Vegas High drink on Friday nights, throwing Teddy Beer cans off the trestle while the Ch-Ch-Chiquitas of LVHS cruise the Spot, in and out of the driveway, circling, trolling.

As me and Shelley turn into the magic driveway under the blinking, rotating sign where the BRIGHT shines brighter than the SPOT, we're looking for the heart of something that probably won't be here until the boys are. We check out who's with who, who's not with who, who's in their own car, who borrowed from M and D. We cruise some more, floating on shock absorbers, big tires, the night pouring into the windows, waiting.

It's 8:45. They're usually back from the Tracks about 9:30. So after we bump over the drive-in's speed traps for the sixth time, we dip into the gutter and out onto Charleston. We head for Fremont Street, past Anderson's Dairy, past the Little Chapel of the West, then turn left onto Fremont, toward the big vortex of light near the Union Pacific depot, the razzle dazzle that never fails to take the words out of my mouth. The Golden Nugget. The Horseshoe. Those zillion bulbs of light.

Shelley switches the station to an oldies show. *Chances Are*, some sixties guy croons as we stop for a red light on Third and Fremont. "My composure sort of ..."

How does somebody's composure sort of slip? I ask Shelley before the singer can finish the sentence. It either does or it doesn't.

True, Shelley says. But Johnny Mathis says so. It must be believed. Funny, Shelley ...

Hey, don't look now, Mattie, but some slime just pulled up next to us on your side of the car.

Some wanna-be Elvis with a souped up Ford idles at the stop light. Come along and be my party doll, he sings like we're his audience. I look at Shelley and roll my eyes. Then I stare straight ahead. He doesn't exist.

Shelley turns up the volume to drown out his, and Johnny's velvet amps my blood and the yearning for the One and Only. I've been waiting for a long time. My hand outside the window can feel the velvet. It tickles the tips of my fingers, the nerve endings. All I can think of is The Man Who Just Might Be Mine, The King.

We cruise past the marquee at the El Portal. *Way Out West*, Shelley says. That's the name of the movie, Mattie. Don't forget it when your mother asks you in the morning. Say it after me. *Way Out West*. She exaggerates her lips.

Way Out West, I mimic her, laughing. Shelley's the best, even if my mother thinks she's a bad influence on her rare gem of a daughter. It's good Shelley isn't afraid of my mother—the Lioness of Righteousness, the Defender of All Virtue. God bless Shelley. The Primo Chiquita.

A car full of shaveheads from Nellis pulls up next to us and pins us with their air force eyes, like we're ground targets in the desert. One whistles a two-finger whistle. Another sticks out his tongue and wiggles it. Yuk, Shelley says. She tries to speed up when the light changes, but the traffic is packed like sardines. She's bumper to bumper with a Dodge wearing Iowa plates.

I've seen enough rubber-neckers from Iowa, she says as she tap dances her foot on the brake.

We're stuck in the intersection, and I feel squirmy like an amoeba under a microscope. Horns honking. Everyone stalled. The Nellis boys next to us, a bunch of prying eyes. I keep my head forward, but notice with my side eyes that one of them is opening the back door of their dull black car and is lunging toward our Plymouth, making like a primate for the entertainment of his friends. I roll up my window and lock my door just before the primate lands on the side of the car and plants a blowfish kiss on the glass. I can hear the rest of the guys in the car laughing like crazy.

Hey girls, he's yelling in between planting slobbery circles across the window. Pussy for me, girls? He puts his hand over his crotch, jiggles his family jewels, sucks in his breath with his teeth tight together.

Don't pay him any attention, I whisper as I turn away from the window, maintaining my cool, hardly breathing.

The blowfish moves over to the windshield and mashes one side of his face against the glass. I act as if I'm talking to Shelley with a permanent left hand angle to my head. He mounts the hood of the car. He's crawling on his hands and knees, panting like a dog in 120-degree heat.

Go find another fireplug, I shout as loud as I can which isn't too loud, then cover my face with the side of my hand. I'm laughing. I shouldn't be.

This isn't all that funny, Shelley says to me. Get off the car, she yells to him. You stupid jerk.

I'm trying to fold up in my elbows and arms, trying to be serious and angry like Shelley, but the flyboy's eyes. They're hollow. There's a famine there.

Luckily, the traffic starts to move, and, as Shelley creeps forward, she hits the brake, hard. He slides back, almost loses his balance, then leaps into the street. He gives us the finger before he becomes a reflection of the flashing lights.

My heart is beating in my throat. There's not enough air in Shelley's car. Shelley, let's get out of here.

Mattie, I'm doing the best I can. One more block.

In one block we'll hit Main Street, the end of Fremont Street, the place where we can turn left and get back to the Bright Spot, where we can hold our breath for something important, like Rod and The King, even though they'll be drunk. Drunk enough to give the finger to all worldly inhabitants plus the moon and the stars as they speed down the highway. Drunk enough to call us Bitch One and Bitch Two.

I love it when they talk like that, words from the Forbidden City. Their words are like bold fingers on my neck, brushing over my breasts, down to my belly button. I can taste their words, and it doesn't matter what they call us, because they need us—our arms, our lips, our necks, our breasts, though we don't plan to give them anything past the neck. We are, after all, Mormon girls in Mormon Levis, saving our sacred bodies for The Big Event called temple marriage.

But just when we turn left onto Main, I feel blood oozing onto my Levis. Oh no, I say to Shelley. My period, right now, right this minute. White Cross Drug, Shelley. Can you believe this happened on Friday night?

Shelley steers the big boaty Plymouth into the parking lot of White Cross Drug. She pulls up next to a long stretched out Cadillac sparkling in the street lights. I crane my head and peer into the car. Some Big Sugar Daddy maybe. I see something sparkling in the back seat, and when the door opens, a showgirl steps out with a cardigan draped over her shoulders. The little sweater doesn't really cover her costume. White satin. A vee down to her navel, big breasts like cantaloupes pushed together. Rhinestones glued over the tops of her eyebrows, eyes smothered with aqua shadow and pencil and mascara, more rhinestones glued to her neck, making two arrows that point to her breasts. Her headdress looks like an albino macaw sprinkled with diamonds.

Wow, I say to Shelley. I'm speechless. I wish I could trade places right this minute, have breasts as big as hers, wrap my head in silken turbans, tie gauzy scarves around my torso every which way.

Stop gawking and go get what you need, Shelley says. We don't have all night, remember. Your mother said twelve sharp, sharp, sharp. She asked me last week to start bringing you home on time. She blames me, your best friend and protector and buddy.

Yes, Sir, I salute her. I feel the crossroads of the seams against my crotch as I push open the door with my shoulder, unfold into the darkening night, step on the asphalt that still holds the heat of the day.

Mother, I think as I look for the right aisle. Ever vigilant Mama mia. Mama owl. I start humming *Stouthearted Men*, her favorite song about men who fight for the right they adore.

The showgirl is standing under the feminine hygiene sign. She has rhinestones down the seams of her white net hose. She must be in between shows. She's picking up a box of Tampax. Wow. Both of us on the same day. The same time. This must be portentous. The Ides of Something. I try not to look at her as she turns back toward the front of the store, but I can't help myself. There's too much to look at.

Up close I can see the lines of things. The outliner on her lips, the eyeliner, the pencilled mole on her cheek. And I'm not sure why, but when she looks at me, I wish she wouldn't have. When she does, I can see two human eyes behind the blinking aqua eyelids. I can see two-in-one people walking down Aisle 5 of the White Cross Drugstore: one underneath a feathered headdress and pushed into surprising places by the limits of the white satin costume, the other looking out at me and wow, do her eyes remind me of my dad talking about the windows of the soul. She's real. Wow. Her eyes briefly graze my face as she passes, leaving me with feelings I don't understand.

After I pay for the pads and push through the glass door, I can't stop thinking about those eyes. Standing alone on the sidewalk, I watch the back end of the long Cadillac flashing its right blinker, halos around the taillights, the body of the Caddy wrapping around the corner and turning right toward The Strip. I think her eyes remind me of the picture of the sad Jesus nailed to the wall of my Sunday school class. Maybe that's blasphemy, Jesus in drag, but he seems to be everywhere, staring out of the strangest places.

Suddenly I feel laced and larded with thoughts of redemption, salvation and eternal life. Maybe Shelley and I should try to get Rod and The King to change their ways: go easy on the beer, be more responsible. She and I are, after all, instruments of God. We don't drink. We don't smoke. We go to church twice on Sunday and once during the week.

But Shelley is honking her horn. Hurry up, she yells out the open window. Let's move. And my ears tune back into Friday night and the strains of *Yellow Submarine* on Shelley's radio. There might be true love waiting for me at the Bright Spot. Remember?

What took you so long? Shelley asks as she turns left onto Las Vegas Boulevard and back toward the Bright Spot.

Slow check-out line, I say. I don't want to talk about the showgirl's eyes. Pull around to the back, some place where it's dark, I say to Shelley. After she does, I unzip my levis, pull down my pants, and safety pin the Kotex to my panties. There's still blood on my Levi's, but it's in a place that shouldn't be noticeable.

What is this yucky stuff anyway that shows up every month? I say to Shelley. And then, without wanting to, even while Shelley's answering me, I'm thinking of Jesus again. Him on the cross. The crown of thorns and pearls of blood on his forehead. And I think of the soldiers staring up at him. And other soldiers carrying shields that aren't big enough to cover their bodies. Arrows. Cannons. War and blood and innocents being massacred. But it's time to hurry up and get back to Friday night. My pants are even tighter when I zip them up again.

I'm ready. Let's hit the Bright Spot, I say, beamingly beamish girl that I am.

You going to buy me some gas for a change? she says, smiling her cheesy smile, her teeth lighting up the car like a neon cheshire cat.

Sure, I say, money being a sore spot between us, me never having anything extra. There's six of us kids and my mother cans every living thing except lizards so we can eat right. How about $2?

Wow, you're loaded, Mattie. Shelley rolls her eyes back and sucks in her cheeks. Her famous fish face.

Don't knock it. It's something.

The jumping neon on the Bright Spot's sign is still going round and round the circular sign. The lights keep traveling the same old same old, and I wonder if there will ever be a moment when something will interfere with this geometrical pattern—six bulbs to a row, each row marching one by one into the light? Could these bulbs ever try another route? Is this world made of uninterruptable patterns? Unleavable sockets? Can anything or anybody dare to be different?

Shelley parks in stall #16. The carhop slides a cardboard ticket under the windshield wiper. Cherry Lime Rickey, we both say in unison. We'd both like to add french-fried onion rings, but we don't have enough money. We don't care about food, anyway. We're still waiting, listening to all the radios as cars cruise the Bright Spot. *You Are So Beautiful. Lady of the Blue Rose.*

When do you think they'll get here? Shelley asks as she guzzles the last of her Cherry-Lime Rickey through her straw. Her red hair reflects the lights on the Bright Spot sign, speckles of light dance across her bangs.

I tap the bottom of my glass to coax the last of the shaved ice to fall in my mouth. They better hurry, I say, getting tough, like I'll leave if they don't show. Fat chance.

And suddenly they're back, leaning into the windows of Shelley's Plymouth. Rod and The King. Their faces are red. They look like they're feelin' good. Park your car, they say. Come with us, you women, you broads.

I gotta take a whiz first, The King says. Too many Teddy Beers. He laughs. He makes a move with his hand like he's gonna whip his jewels out from behind his zipper right then and there and do it in the bright lights. But he winks at me and walks off for the bathroom. He's so lanky and tall and knows how to move those thin hips of his. I'm holding my breath again. Hurry back, I whisper, then think about the science of pelvises.

Too much hard work at the Tracks, Rod says as we walk toward The King's car. Lifting those cans takes a lot of muscle. Like Olympic weight lifters, you better believe.

As soon as The King returns, we all slip into the magic car, the silver streak, Shelley and I in the back seat, Rod at shotgun, The King driving. I wish I was up there with him. I'd slide so close to him, I'd barely leave him room. I want body contact. But instead I watch the back of his head as he drives, the steady rhythm of the street lights lighting up his olive neck, his dark hair like a Bedouin's, the perfect desert boyfriend, someone who might ride a camel and wrap scarves around his head if he had some.

Why don't you get your ten-pound weakling body to the gym? The King is shouting to Rod as we pass Health World, the new gym in town, punching him in the shoulder.

Muscles, Rod says as he pushes a beer can against his bicep. The only kind of muscle I need, he says.

The King is slapping the seat with his hand. He's laughing as if Rod just told the last joke on earth. He's punching his buddy in the arm and the car is running on auto-pilot.

Watch where you're going, I want to say, but don't. I bite my tongue. I want to fit this time and this moment. Our Mutual Improvement Association teachers gave us cards that said "Dare to Be Different." They thought this would encourage us to be daring enough not to fall into the morass of the world and the pit of the hell-bound, daring enough to live by The Truth. But I took the cards to mean I should be different from the way anybody told me I had to live life. Dare to be different from everything.

So I don't care if our car is weaving slightly as The King drives from street light to street light. Life is to be lived now, so why spend it preparing for the next one, hoping I'll be God's Little Darlin'? He holds the steering wheel with two thumbs, and I wish again I could be by his shoulder and see into the night better than I can from the back seat.

The stars are shining more brightly the farther we pull away from the center of Las Vegas.

Where are we going? I ask as I lean on my elbows against the front seat.

The Lake, The King says. Something new.

What would really be new, I say, is to drive to the stars.

Well, aren't you something? The King says to me.

Did my voice sound sexy when I said "stars?" I wonder. Is that what he means? Or does he think it's a cool idea to drive to the stars? When we get to the lake, maybe he'll want to change places with Shelley. Sit in the back seat with me.

Today's the day, Rod sings, the Teddy Beers have their picnic.

Tonight's the night, I say.

The radio blasts as we whip down Boulder Highway toward the man-made lake called Mead which buries skeletons of Moapa Indians and Mormon pioneers and the bones of their houses. I've heard about this in Sunday school. The King accelerates. I close my eyes and imagine we could leave the ground any minute and take an aerial highway and blast through the stringy night clouds highlighted by the moon. I feel the power of speed, the moan of the tires spinning faster than light traveling.

I look over at my best friend Shelley whose jaw is tight. We both laugh, and yet steel-nerve Shelley's gripping the seat with claw-like hands. Her face looks white in this light. The desert hills whip by like ghosts, the marker posts by the sides of the road, white dominoes falling behind the path of the car. *Chances Are*, I hum.

I like the idea of leaving the ground, leaving my father's Dale Carnegie and Norman Vincent Peale speeches. He won't allow me to say anything unkind about someone unless I say three nice things. We live The Golden Rule at home. We believe in all good things, we seek after these things. Life is one big bud of goodness, I've been told, and yet, sometimes it's a maximum security prison to have to smile and be loving all the time. To be inside those invisible bars of goodness that catch sunlight and keep me true to my word, true to the covenants with God. A cage of golden sunlight, golden plates, and golden birds who can't sing because their feathers are solid. Golden angels who can't fly because they're made of gold.

I think of myself giving my testimony in sacrament meeting. "I know this church is the only true church on the face of the earth and that Joseph Smith is the Only True Prophet." Believing, believing, and yet here I am, the velour air rubbing across my face and arms and making me want to unbutton my shirt. Open up to the night air. Save me, somebody.

Maybe tonight we'll bust free to the new religion of time and space. We're going fast enough. Fly, King, I whisper so he can't hear me. Step on the accelerator. My veins are drunk with you.

Have a swig, Rod says, reaching across the seat and handing his Teddy Beer to The King. He takes a long swig and heads into the night.

Shelley and I are leaning against the back seat, our legs spread wide. I'm looking at two large white Vs. Our legs in the shadow of the car. Our legs that look like bones in this moonlight. I love the wind that's whipping my hair and tangling it and blinding me with its thickness. Hair in my mouth, whipping around my ears. Hair is the only thing I can feel right now. Sometimes it slaps my cheek and stings, but I like the almost feel of cutting into my innocent skin. I'm a pharisee. A whited sepulchre in white Levis. Me. I touch my mouth. It can't wait until we stop somewhere so it can kiss The King. French kiss him. Feel his tongue in my mouth. It can't wait to be bruised from kissing too hard, and I feel throbbing against the tight seam between my legs. Our bodies will wrangle with each other, roll on some sand at the lake, though I know it's only a rocky beach. I can't wait for him to get hard and push against me and my pelvis bone and the cloth of the Mormon Levis.

But I know I'm still a good girl. I want to live with Jesus some day. Shelley, too. We're saving ourselves like stamps or coins or something valuable, even though we're crashing through the night, headlights cutting the dark into ribbons. I have a hunch we're both thinking that some day soon we'll be more careful. Do what our parents ask us. But this Nevada night. It sucks us in like a Hoover, and we're on the edge of something big.

The King takes another sip of the beer, tossing his head back for one second too long. The car swerves onto the gravelly shoulder of the road and fishtails from side to side. Careening, lurching, jerking, tipping, swaying, righting itself. The King finally gets control and pulls the silver Pontiac back into the southbound lane of the two-lane highway. We're still headed south. Both Shelley and I have one hand flat against our chests. With the other hand, we're holding each other's arms tighter than a fistful of cash.

Damn, that was beautiful, Rod says. Damn, damn. He's slapping his knees and pulling the ring top of another beer. Sweet little Teddy Beer, he says. Good little Teddy. Take care of me. Make me happy. He's stroking the side of the can as if it were a stuffed animal he had when he was a kid.

Give me another sip, The King says. Rod reaches across the front seat, his arm silhouetted against the windshield and the passing rocks and hills that look like grotesque shapes of elephants and desert camels we're passing on the lake road. Beer, beer, wonderful beer, he chants while The King takes more time with this swig. The King accelerates even more. We're heading for a rise in the road, the mound of the railroad track looming large ahead of us, and suddenly the sharp definition of double yellow stripes seems to be rising straight up to the sky.

Jesus and Mary, Rod says. Holy shit! Will you look at that Monster Rise in the Road? Holy holy shit. Rod's eyes are big as he holds his beer can mid-air and looks at The King with a mouth caught by the hook of surprise.

Hey you women back there, The King is yelling. You want love, do you? You want excitement? Well, hold onto your seats. We're gonna take air. A little foreplay, girls and boys.

Floor it, Rod says, leaning into the windshield to watch the ground rise. Go for it.

Maybe we'll sail when we hit the top of the mound because our car isn't a car anymore. I look at Shelley who looks back at me. Our faces are blanks. We're here. On the ride. We accept our fate as The King steps on the pedal, pushes it to the floor, and we head for the high point in the road, the place with a railroad cross shining back at us. The radio is blasting.

I grab Shelley's hand and hold it tight and together we lay our heads back and surrender, just like we used to do on the Roll-O-Plane at the carnival. Maybe we'll land like a jet on the other side. Maybe we'll keep flying. If that's the case, maybe Jesus will be waiting for us with open arms.

I squeeze my eyes shut. I squeeze Shelley's hand and brace my feet against the floor. I love you, Shelley, I whisper. You're my best friend ever. If I don't have anything else that matters, I have you.

You're the best, Shelley says, wrinkling her nose as she squeezes her eyes tightly. I peek at the black mountain of road soaring in front of the headlights, then slam my eyes shut again.

Jesus, we just might be coming to you. Hold those arms wide open. We're leaving the desert and maybe we'll get to look into your eyes and see if they really are sad, and if they are, we can ask you why.

Epilogue: Origins

"The Whip" is based on an anecdote found in the archives of the Fife Mormon Collection, Fife Folklore Archives, Utah State University, Logan, Utah. This tale was related by Mrs. Syrena Lowe from Franklin, Idaho, on May 17, 1946, to Hector Lee and Austin and Alta Fife. "My grandmother, Elvira Wheeler Rockwood, was coming across the plains, and for some reason Rockwood gave her a licking with his ox whip, and when he came in for supper she had some soup for him and he says, 'Elvira, what is this you've got for my supper?' 'The same thing I had for breakfast!' She'd cut his whip up and made soup from it. ... She left Rockwood after she got to Salt Lake, and married again."

"Spirit Babies" comes from talk I heard as a child and as a married woman from various Mormon women in small group conversations. They reported dreams where a spirit "came" to them and said it wanted to be born to their particular families.

"Wild Sage" comes from an incident reported by Al Curtis of Logan, Utah, when he was approximately eighty years old. It was recorded by Austin and Alta Fife and can be found in the Fife Mormon Collection, Fife Folklore Archives. "My father was on a mission in England. He was sick and there didn't seem to be anything they could do for him. Mother said that we would have a special prayer one night so that he would be able to fulfill his mission. That very night the Three Nephites came to my room. It was as bright as day, and they told me what to do. They said if I would go up and gather wild sage and send it to him, and tell him to make a tea and drink it he would get well. I did that. I sent it to him ... and he made the tea and drank it and was well again." Curtis described the Three Nephites as being "all in white robes, clean shaven. They looked very similar to each other, like brothers. Their skin was rather dark. They talked to me and told me my mission was to be like theirs, and it has been true. I have never been on a mission but I have made converts everywhere I have went." Fife cites documentary evidence that the belief in the intercession of the Three Nephites was well established in Utah in 1851. The origin of the Three Nephites is from Book of Mormon scripture. Three disciples of Jesus Christ (when he appeared in the Americas) wanted to live forever: "And when he had spoken unto them, he turned himself unto the three, and said unto them: What will ye that I should do unto you, when I am gone unto the Father? And they sorrowed in their hearts, for they durst not speak unto him the thing which they desired. And he said unto them: Behold, I know your thoughts, and ye have desired the thing which John, my beloved, who was with me in my ministry, before that I was lifted up by the Jews, desired of me. Therefore, more blessed are ye, for ye shall live to behold all the doings of the Father unto the children of men, even until all things shall be fulfilled according to the will of the Father, when I shall come into my glory with the powers of heaven. And ye shall never endure the pains of death; but when I shall come in my glory ye shall be changed in the twinkling of an eye from mortality to immortality ... " (3 Ne. 28:4-8).

"The Boy and the Hand" has its origins in a retold story from James M. Fife, who heard the original in a testimony meeting in Lincoln, Idaho, when a Mrs. Kelley got up and bore her testimony. According to the Fife Mormon Collection, Mrs. Kelley said that "one of the children had gotten a fish bone in its throat and was about to choke to death. She saw a mysterious hand, just as plainly as she could see her own hand, reach into the child's mouth and extract the fish bone, thus saving the child from death."

"Devil Horse" has it roots in a story from my family history found in "A Sketch of the Life of Jonathan Calkins Wright," written and self-published by his son, Brigham Wright, and dated March 8, 1931. An excerpt:

"But when (missionary) Lyman asked him to accept a Book of Mormon, he did so, and as soon as Lyman had left, father commenced to read. Bed time came but still he read. Finally he said to his wife, Rebecca, 'I must see this man, Joseph Smith.' 'I wish you would,' she replied, 'if you don't you'll go crazy.'

"As soon as he was able, father got on his horse and started for Nauvoo [Illinois], some eighty miles away. He rode early and late, and it was necessary for him to bate the horse. When he did this he took the saddle off, got his book and read it as he waited. Every minute he had he devoted to reading the Book of Mormon. He hadn't read a great deal of it until he found something that didn't suit him. He shut the book with a bang and said, 'I'll not go another step. I'm going right home. I don't believe the story.' His horse was standing off a little way, and as Wright approached the animal, it started for him with its mouth wide open in a most vicious manner. Seemed determined to fight him. It whirled and kicked him, then broke loose and ran away. 'I knew in a minute that the devil had taken possession of my horse,' father said."

Jonathan Calkins Wright was converted to the restored gospel and was baptized by Hyrum Smith, Joseph Smith's older brother (Joseph Smith was in Pennsylvania at the time), in the Mississippi River around the year 1840.

"Ida's Sabbath" was inspired by an act of nature in the late 1980s—lightning striking and destroying a steeple of an LDS wardhouse in Salt Lake City (3900 South and 2000 East streets), near my home at the time.

"Dust to Dust" originated from a story told by a woman attending a lecture I was giving at the University of Utah. I asked if people in the audience remembered stories passed down from their ancestors. This woman volunteered that her grandmother, who lived in southern Utah, had been visited once by an ornate golden carriage and a man dressed in satin breeches who asked her for money.

"The Fiddler and the Wolf" is adapted from an incident related by Mary Hilton of Ogden, Utah, on August 26, 1946, to Austin E. Fife, recorded in the Fife Mormon Collection. The fiddler in this case was called Uncle Tom, who lived and played for dances in Weber County, Utah. One night Uncle Tom couldn't get through the snow drifts, so he "cut back over across the Weber River and started down through the river bottoms by Wilson Lane." When the wolves followed him, he found refuge in a cabin where the "McFarland boys had boiled their molasses called the Old Molasses House," and he climbed the chimney after discovering a window had been removed. In this incident a search party finds him alive just after he's played "Turkey in the Straw" to "charm the wolves." The searchers kill one of the animals, the rest of the wolves run away, and a report of the number of tracks around the cabin said there were seventeen wolves in the pack. A relative of Mrs. Hilton, Robert McFarland, was purported to have the wolf skin "in front of their old stove."

"Bread for Gunnar" was inspired by a fragment found at the Utah Historical Society Library, recorded by William Mulder, about a Scandinavian man in Salt Lake City who continually repainted his house and covered his chimney with decorative tin and bouquets of paper flowers.

"A Brief History of Seagulls: A Trilogy with Notes" is based on an event in Utah history—the 1848 arrival of seagulls who saved the first Utah pioneers' spring crops during a plague of crickets. A friend told me of her great-great-grandmother who had the first lace curtains in Salt Lake city and how they were devoured by crickets. Part II of the story was seeded by an article in the *Salt Lake Tribune*—"Mormon Crickets Threaten Utah Cropland," by Robert Green, May 6, 1990, especially by the paragraph that reads: "Here their numbers are so vast that seagulls quickly eat their fill and spend most of their time napping on sandbars." Part III drew its inspiration from a news story in May 1982 about an F-16 fighter jet on a training mission from Hill Air Force Base. The jet crashed into the Great Salt Lake after a collision with a seagull crippled its engines. Further information was taken from Paul Rolly's article in the *Salt Lake Tribune*, "Utah's Bird Becoming a Nuisance," August 8, 1986. He reported measures being taken against the seagulls by the U.S. Air Force (BASH—Bird Air Strike Hazard program since 1975). At the time of the article, gulls were considered the biggest problem bird by the Air Force, according to Captain Russell DeFusco, Tyndall Air Force Base, Florida, the air force losing twenty-three jets in fifteen years to bird collisions.

"Prophet by the Sea" was inspired by an article by Ferren L. Christensen in "Compassion of a President," *Ensign* 9 (Jan. 1979): 69-79.

"Mormon Levis" was written in 1995 when I was asked for a story about Mormons in Nevada by anthologist Kathryn Wilder. It reflects my lifelong fascination with the sacred and the profane—something that appears so obvious in a city the likes of Las Vegas (my home from 1954 to 1964).